TACKLING LIFE

KATHLEEN KELLY

Tackling Life

Kathleen Kelly

Copyright © 2021 Kathleen Kelly

All Rights Reserved

All efforts have been made to ensure the correct grammar and punctuation in the book. If you do find any errors, please e-mail Kathleen Kelly: kathleenkellyauthor@gmail.com

Thank you.

Disclaimer: The material in this book contains graphic language and sexual content and is intended for mature audiences, ages 18 and older.

Table of Contents

Editing by Swish Design & Editing[1]
Proofreading by Swish Design & Editing[2]
Book design by Swish Design & Editing[3]
Cover design by Clarise Tan of CT Creations[4]
Cover Image Copyright 2021
First Edition 2021
All Rights Reserved

1. http://www.swishgrafix.com.au

2. http://www.swishgrafix.com.au

3. http://www.swishgrafix.com.au

4. https://www.facebook.com/groups/CTCeations/

BLURB

Grayson Moore linebacker for the New England Warriors. His entire life has been working up to this moment, the moment when his team wins the Super Bowl.

But life has a way of throwing you an illegal pass.

Diandra Evergrow was the love of his life, well, until she ended it.

Now she's walked back in on the best night of his life with news that could destroy not only him but all those who are close to him.

Will Grayson put it all on the line for the woman who once claimed his heart?

Or will he tuck and run to protect it?

Book 2 in Kathleen Kelly's Sports Romance Series.

For everyone who enjoyed the first book, Tackling Love, this one is for you.

TABLE OF CONTENTS

PROLOGUE

GRAYSON

The music is pumping as I enter the club. I'm high-fiving people as I make my way through the crowd of partygoers. Everyone is in good spirits. The New England Warriors have won the Super Bowl. It's a dream come true for me, something I've worked toward my entire life.

Colton Anders, our quarterback and my best friend, is at the bar with my teammates. His woman, Skye, is only a few feet away, staring at him like he's hung the moon.

Walking up to Colton, I slap him on the back, and he turns to shake my hand then pulls me in for the briefest of hugs.

"I can't believe we did it!" I yell as I turn around, arms in the air, doing a victory spin.

"Me, either."

I'm grinning at Colton, but he's not smiling, his expression is serious. There's not even a hint of happiness or excitement.

"Not Skye problems?" I ask in a hushed tone.

"No, no, no. Syke is perfect. We're good." He licks his lips in nervousness.

"What then?"

Colton takes a deep breath. "You have a visitor."

Laughing, I slap his shoulder. "I bet I'll have *a lot* of visitors in the off-season." I wink at him.

Colton doesn't return my teasing. In fact, he looks uncomfortable.

"Is my mom here?"

Colton smiles. "No, Gray." He lets out a sigh and shakes his head. "It's Diandra."

I shake my head twice and do a double-take. "Diandra?"

"Yeah, she's over near Skye."

Turning, Diandra's standing slightly behind Colt's woman. I can't believe I didn't notice her. She's still gorgeous. Her mocha-colored skin glows next to her figure-hugging gold dress. Those blue eyes, which still haunt me, are staring back at me. Why couldn't she have put on a ton of weight or have severe acne? An ache in my chest intensifies the longer I stare at her.

Colton nudges me, drawing my attention back to him. "You okay?"

"I feel like I've been sucker-punched on the best night of my life." Puffing out my cheeks, I let out a breath. "Why is she here?"

Colton clears his throat and shakes his head. "You know I love you like a brother, but she needs to tell you."

Placing my hands on my hips, I look down. "Whatever she has to say, she's three years too late. *I don't care.*"

"*You will.*"

"Fine."

Turning, I stride toward her. Skye moves out of the way and hurries toward Colton, giving me the briefest of smiles. Diandra has her hands clasped together in front of her, a worried expression on her still-beautiful face.

"Hello, Gray."

The ache in my chest expands, and I rub it to try and dissipate the pressure. "Hello, Diandra. What do you want?" The worlds come out quickly and far harsher than I imagined they would.

She hurt me so badly when she ended us. Diandra picked up and moved to New York. She told me not to follow, that it was over—no explanation, no further contact, nothing. I was messed up and not in a good way for a long time. I'm only just dating again. Sure, I have hook-ups but nothing serious. To say Diandra broke my heart doesn't seem like a powerful enough statement. No, she shattered it into a million pieces.

Diandra lets out a huff, clearly not expecting me to be so aggressive. "Don't be like that, Gray."

"We just won the Super Bowl. It's the best night of my life in a very long time, and you turn up. Why? Did you want to wreck this for me too?"

Diandra steps back as though I've hit her, and instantly I regret my words. She bends, picks up her purse, and walks past me as though I don't exist. Briefly, she stops and says something to Colton, whose eyes come to me with a look of surprise, and then she continues through the throng of people and out of the club.

Colton walks toward me. "*You* fucked up."

"*I* fucked up?" I shake my head at him. "Do you remember how she treated me? And you're telling me *I* fucked up."

"I get it, Gray, she hurt you, but trust me when I tell you, you need to hear what she has to say."

Shaking my head, I wave a hand at him. "Nah, not tonight. Tonight we celebrate." I grin at him, projecting a false bravado that I don't feel now having upset Diandra. "If it's so important, I'll ring her tomorrow."

Colton nods. "Okay, just make sure you do."

I crack an eye open, and the light causes a blinding headache. With a groan, I roll over and put my feet on the floor. Looking at the carpet, I must be in a hotel room, a suite. I have no idea how I got here. No one shares my bed. Tentatively, I stand and stumble into the bathroom. Turning on the faucet, I fill up the sink and splash cold water onto my face, feeling instantly better.

The man staring back at me in the mirror is a joke. I'm not one for drinking so much, I believe my body is my temple, but seeing Diandra rocked me to my core. She's still able to unnerve me. There's an aura around her, and she's like a magnet, pulling people into her stratosphere. Clearly, Colton thinks I need to go back to where my world revolves around her, but I've grown in the past three years. I'm stronger, my career path is mapped out, and I don't have time for trivial pursuits.

My cell phone rings, and I ignore it. My priority is to shower, clean up, and then I'll think about food and then maybe Diandra.

Who am I kidding?

I have no intention of calling her. With that thought, I step into the shower. The spray is nice and cold as the water runs over me, helping to clear my addled mind. If this doesn't help sober me up, nothing will. My headache slowly eases, making me feel a hundred times better. I soap up, then stand under the spray until my fingers prune.

With a sigh and a shake of my head, I get out of the shower, towel myself off, and go in search of my clothes. They're neatly folded on the couch in the adjoining room.

"Hello?" I call out, but there's no one else here.

So, I put on the same clothes as last night and head downstairs to the lobby.

The concierge greets me, "Hello, Mr. Moore. I trust the room was to your liking?"

Frowning, I ask, "It was a great room, but how did I get here?"

He smiles. "You arrived by cab, and I helped you to your room."

Awkwardly I ask, "Was I alone?"

"Completely, sir."

Relief floods through me, and my cell phone rings again. Taking it out of my pocket, Colton's name flashes on the screen. I hit the decline button and then notice he's rung me five times. Jesus, he's like a dog with a bone.

With my focus back on the concierge, I ask, "Do I owe you anything?"

"No, sir, you're paid in full."

With a grateful smile, I walk away and out into the sunlight. I wish I had my sunglasses as the bright light causes me to squint.

"Look, Mom, it's Grayson Moore!" shouts a boy from a few feet away.

I smile and wave and keep walking. I love the fans, but right now, I need to find food. Hailing a cabbie, he pulls up next to me, and I climb in.

"Where to?"

"1502 Possum Road, Weston."

"You sure, buddy? It's a bit out of town."

"I have family there."

The cabbie's lips turn down, but he pulls out into traffic. He must not be a football fan as he doesn't make small talk for the ride out to my mother's, which is fine by me as the headache from earlier is thumping along nicely with every bump and rut in the road.

Mom's house is a little over half an hour away. I spend the time thinking about the last game, the one where we won. A smile creeps its way across my face, then Diandra's face flashes into focus and my smile disappears.

The cabbie pulls up in my mother's driveway. The fare is a little over forty dollars, so I give him sixty and get out. Before I can knock on the door, my mother opens it.

"Hey, Mom!" I embrace her. "We won!"

"I know, honey." She pulls back from me, not letting me enter her house.

"Mom?"

She puts her arms across the doorway. "There's someone here."

I stand back and give her a cheeky grin. "You got a man in there?"

Mom smiles. "No, honey. Diandra is here."

This takes me by surprise, and whatever she sees in my face, Mom drops her arms, and I enter her home. It's a ranch-style house she's recently redecorated in what she calls Hamptons' bling. To me, it looks as though she's only changed the color scheme to white, blue, and lots of crystal chandeliers, but I'm no expert. It's a far cry from the crappy apartment she used to live in years ago. This was my gift to Mom for all her hard work and support back in the early days.

Sitting at my mother's dining table in a cream pant suit with a blue silk blouse is Diandra. At first, she looks shocked to see me, and then she slowly rises.

"I told you, I had to speak to you, Gray. I thought your mom might break the ice."

Mom puts a hand on my arm. "Do you need something to eat?"

"Yes, and Advil."

Mom squeezes me and leaves us.

"Gray—"

I shake my head. "Whatever you have to say, Diandra, can wait until I've had something to eat."

Her lips press together, and she clenches her jaw. "Fine."

Diandra walks into the kitchen, and like a lost puppy, I trail behind her.

Mom is putting together the makings of a grilled cheese which isn't like her. Normally, she'd make me fried chicken, so whatever Diandra has to tell me must be bad.

I sit at the island counter, and Mom puts a bottle of Advil and a glass of water in front of me. "Take them," she orders.

Considering I asked for them, her request feels redundant. I take two then swivel to look at Dee—that's what I called her way back when.

"Do you want one, too, Diandra?" asks my mom, gesturing toward the food.

"No, thank you, Minerva."

"Coffee?"

"Yes," we both say at the same time.

Mom smiles. "I'll put the machine on." She makes a fuss of turning on the machine and then looks at me. "Diandra has something to tell you."

"Then let *her* tell it."

"Grayson Moore, don't you use that tone with me." Mom puts her hands on her hips and waves a teaspoon at me.

Speaking through clenched teeth and with forced restraint, I nod at her. "Yes, ma'am."

Mom makes us all a coffee and puts one in front of me. Diandra's she leaves on the kitchen island nearest to where she's standing. With a sigh, I stare at Diandra as she picks up the cup. Mom puts the grilled cheese in front of me, and I take a bite.

"Why are you *here*?" I ask with a full mouth.

Diandra puts down her cup and glances at my mother, who nods at her. "I want to start out by apologizing to you and your mother." She straightens up and undoes the button on her jacket, then takes a deep breath. "You have a son... his name is Dawson."

Dropping the grilled cheese and swallowing down the food which feels like a large brick, I stare at my Mom, who nods, smiling, but she has tears in her eyes.

"*I* have a son?"

"*We* have a son."

I bark out a mirthless laugh. "Now, I get it. You think because we won the Super Bowl that you can waltz in here looking for a payday?"

"Grayson!" admonishes my mother.

"Not going to happen, sweetheart. Let's do a paternity test first, and we'll see *if* he's mine."

Diandra holds up a hand to my mother, a frozen smile on her face. "It's okay, Minerva, I deserved that." She turns to me. "I don't want your *money*, Gray. If that were the case, I'd have hit you up for child support years ago. Did you notice I gave him your grandfather's name?"

I shrug. "If you're not here for money, why are you here?"

My mother takes two quick steps toward me and slaps her hand on the kitchen island, and the sound reverberates around the room. "Because in times of trouble, family sticks together!"

"Mom, how can you say that? *If* he's mine, we'll work out a payment plan and go from there."

"Grayson Moore, I raised you better than that!" Mom puts her hands on her hips. "Diandra is here because the boy is sick, and you might be the only one who can help him."

Diandra sits beside me. "He has Goodpasture Syndrome. It's rare for a child under four to get it, only a handful have. He's in remission right now but needs a kidney transplant. I'm not a great match. We need to test you to see if you are." She sucks in a breath and lets it out slowly. "Of course, it all depends *if* you are his father. They'll need to do a paternity test to see."

Her words cut through me like a knife. It's one thing for me to insinuate he isn't mine and totally another for her to imply she fooled around.

"When do I need to do this?"

"Yesterday," Diandra replies.

"I'll get tested, too," says Mom.

"Where?" I ask.

"He's in a private hospital in New York. I'd like it if we could leave immediately." She smiles. "I don't like to be away from him this long."

Mom is wringing her hands, her expression anxious.

"Would you have told me about him if he wasn't sick?"

Diandra shakes her head. "I don't know. What you and I had feels like a lifetime ago. I've made a new life for myself, one where Dawson is my priority. My life consists of Dawson and work. There's no room for anything else."

"You could've told me." Feelings of hurt rise to the surface. With her sitting so close to me, all I can think is that I loved her. She was my everything.

"You had a plan. Gray, you said a child would ruin everything, so I did what I felt was right for the both of us. Look where you are, you're on track, you've achieved so much. We were too young to take on the responsibility of a child."

"So you did it on your own?"

Diandra exchanges a glance with my mom.

"Gray, none of this matters. The only thing that matters is you have a son, a son who needs our help. Let's get tested, and we'll go from there. You might not even be a match." Mom smiles encouragingly at me.

Diandra is nodding. Clearly, these two have come to an agreement. One where I should just go along with whatever they say.

A son.

Diandra reaches out to touch me, then pulls back as though some hidden force is stopping her. "Please, Gray."

With both hands, I rub my face several times, then sigh. "Okay, let's do this. I need to go home and get some clothes."

"I'm booked on a flight in two hours." Diandra glances at my mother. "Minerva has all the details. You can stay with me while you're in town." She reaches across, and this time she squeezes my hand, causing an electric current to run up my arm. Diandra must feel it, too, for she quickly moves away, rubbing her hands together. "Thank you, Gray. I know it's a lot to take in."

"Does he know who I am?"

Diandra nods. "Yes, he knows you're his dad. He follows the New England Warriors, well he follows all of the teams, but he knows you play for them. He'll have been super excited that you won."

My mother hugs Diandra and sees her to the door, leaving me to fester.

A son.

Named after my grandfather, no less.

Mom walks back into the kitchen. "What are you waiting for?"

"He might not be mine."

Mom shakes her head. "I saw photos, and he's the spitting image of you at his age."

Guilt washes through me. I hadn't thought to ask for pictures.

"You could be seeing what you want to see."

Mom puts an arm around me. "Would it be so bad if you had a son?"

I shake my head. "No, Mom. It's having that woman back in my life."

"I seem to remember you loved *that woman* very much." Mom lets me go and moves to the other end of the house, where her bedroom is located. I finish my sandwich, then stand and follow her.

"You don't need to come," I say as I enter her bedroom.

"What if you're not a match?" she asks, putting clothes into a carry-on.

"Again, Mom, he might not be mine."

"Pfft!" she replies, waving a hand at me. "We'll find out soon enough."

CHAPTER 1

GRAYSON

Five Years Earlier

A blind date. My mother set me up on a blind date. I don't have time for distractions. My life revolves around football and college. That's all.

This girl is the daughter of one of my mother's friends, and she's just transferred to my school. Upon hearing this, Mom volunteered me as a chaperone to show her around for the night. She knew I was going to a party at one of the frat houses. It's not like I let loose very often. I'm focused. Having to babysit some female, who obviously can't get a date for herself, isn't how I planned this evening.

Sitting out in front of her apartment, I wish I could drive away, but my mother would whoop my ass. Sighing, I open the door to my old beat-up Honda and get out. It's a nice neighborhood. Just off campus—her parents must have money.

There's no doorman, but there's an intercom. I hit the buzzer.

"Hello?" She sounds breathless.

"Hello, I'm Grayson Moore. I'm here for a Dianne?"

"Diandra," she corrects me.

"Aww, geez, sorry. Diandra. My mom got your name wrong."

In truth, *I* got the name wrong. I knew it started with a D, and that's about it.

Laughter answers me as the door buzzes, allowing me to enter. Her apartment is on the ground floor. I rap my knuckles on her door, and she opens it immediately.

Diandra has long, dark curly hair, amazing blue eyes, and is wearing a little black dress with six-inch high heels. The woman is gorgeous. This is no wilderbeast desperate for a date, she's a goddess in search of worshippers.

She cocks her head to the side and gestures for me to come in. "Hello, Grayson." Her voice washes over me like silk.

I stumble past her, and she giggles.

"Are you okay?"

"You're gorgeous," I blurt, then instantly regret it.

Diandra stands in the open doorway, looking surprised. "What were you expecting?" She laughs. "Did my mother describe me as an ogre? Or a humpback? Or..." She draws out the last word.

Holding up my hands in an apology, I say, "No, no, no!" I shake my head. "It's all on me. I assumed because you couldn't get a date that you were—" Realizing what I'm saying, I stop myself. My face is burning, and I wish the floor would open up and swallow me whole.

Diandra laughs. "Well, your mom told my mom that you were a handsome gentleman who needed to have some fun."

She shuts the door and walks past, winking at me. "But not *too* much fun."

"I'm so sorry."

Diandra turns, a scowl on her face that turns into a grin. "Don't be. It's always nice to receive a compliment and to be told I'm..." she does inverted commas in the air, "... dateable."

Nervously, I laugh. Diandra is confident. I like it.

"Do you want a drink?"

"No, I'm not drinking."

A frown furrows her brow. "You don't drink?"

I smile. "No, I do. But I've got a game this week, so I need to keep in top shape. No drinking."

"No late nights, either?" Diandra asks as she picks up a glass filled with red wine and takes a sip.

Trying to laugh it off, I nod and make light of it. "Great first date, huh? No drinking and home in bed by ten."

Diandra smiles. "First date? What makes you think you're getting a second date, Grayson Moore?" she replies, in a lighthearted, teasing tone.

I grin at her. "I've got a good feeling about you."

A giggle escapes her, and she puts the wine glass down. "Come on, let's get to the party."

Suddenly, I don't like the idea of sharing her with a crowd of people.

"How about we go out to dinner instead? There's a place not too far from here."

Diandra eyes me cautiously. "Dinner?" I nod. "Okay, so long as we go dutch."

I shake my head. "My momma would throttle me if she knew a lady paid her way on a date."

She giggles again. "Okay, dinner sounds good. I haven't eaten since this morning."

"How come?"

"I have a part-time job at an accounting firm." Diandra stops herself, closes her eyes, and holds up a hand. "That sounded way more impressive than it should have. I do all the crappy jobs no one wants to do, but I'm learning a lot. It also means that sometimes, I work through lunch so I have everything ready for the afternoon. I'm trying to make myself indispensable to them."

"You're studying accounting?"

She nods. "I love numbers, always have." Diandra picks up her purse. "You're on a football scholarship, right?"

"Yeah. There's no way I'd be able to afford to go if I wasn't."

Diandra is holding her clutch with both hands in front of her. "Should we go?" she asks with a shrug.

"Sure."

She walks to her front door, opens it, and steps out into the hallway. While she's locking up, I rush to the building's door and hold it open for her. Diandra gives me a huge smile as she passes through, then I rush to my car so I can get the door.

Diandra stops in front of my trusty Honda and looks at me sideways. "Are you sure you can pay for dinner?"

Leaning an arm across the door of my car, I move slightly toward. her. "*Never* judge a man by his car."

Her lips go into a firm line as she tries to suppress her laughter. "Right. Got it."

She climbs in, and those lips turn up in a smile. I rush around to the driver's side and get in, eager to spend more time with her.

"It's safe, right?" Diandra teases.

"Hey! My baby is perfectly safe."

As if to embarrass me, my car backfires, and Diandra jumps. Her eyes go wide, and she grips the passenger side armrest. "Perfectly safe?"

Pulling out into traffic, I laugh. "Mostly."

I have exactly twenty-two dollars and thirty-eight cents in my wallet.

Dinner?

What the hell was I thinking?

Driving down by the river, I park a little way from the bridge and as close to our destination as I can. With those heels on, I'm not sure how far she can walk, so best to be cautious. Having a single mother raise you, you learn from an early age what women will and won't do. My mom has shoes that are only good for sitting in and looking good, not walking long distances.

"There's a restaurant near here?"

I nod. "It's not far."

Diandra tilts her head to the side. "My mother and your mother know I'm with you."

My eyebrows draw together, and I'm sure my face is a mask of confusion. "And?"

"If you're planning on killing me, you'll get caught."

Laughter rumbles up out of my chest. "It's Friday night and not a full moon, so you're safe."

Diandra links her arm with mine and laughs. "Good to know."

Together we walk along the river, the lights of the city reflecting off its surface. In the distance is a food truck, and I guide her toward it.

"Do you enjoy going to school here?"

I nod. "Yeah. It's a nice city. The people are friendly, and the campus is great."

"I've been here for three months, but with working and classes, I haven't explored the city properly."

"Wait, I thought you just moved here?"

Diandra blushes and scrunches her eyebrows. "I have a confession to make."

"You're married with three kids and a dog?" I tease.

She shakes her head. "I've been to a couple of your games, and when I found out that my mom knew yours..."

Unlinking my arm from hers, I stand in front of her. "Wait, you organized this?"

"Yeah," she admits, looking at the ground.

"And *you* wanted to meet *me*?"

There's a smile on her lips, and Diandra looks me in the eyes. "Yes, I did."

I shake my head in disbelief. "I might be a serial killer, but *you* sound like a stalker."

Diandra laughs, and her embarrassment vanishes. "We make an awesome pair."

Linking my arm back through hers, I point at the food truck. "Best hotdogs in town."

Diandra smiles. "I love hotdogs. You're going to be harshly judged if they don't stack up."

Walking up to the van, the owner, Bruno, leans out and yells a greeting, "Hey, Gray! You want your usual?"

"Make it two."

Bruno gives me the thumbs up and gets to work. He has party lights set up at night and a few tables. It's early, so there aren't many people around. Later, when they've had too much to drink, they'll stumble to Bruno's for a hot meal. It's well-known in the area as the place to go. I like it as Bruno always has a story to share, and it's not expensive. Not that I've ever taken a date here before.

"So, you're a regular?"

"Yeah," I admit, as we sit at one of the tables. "I promise it's good, and I hope you don't mind me ordering for us both."

"I'm curious to see what your *usual* is."

Smiling, I ask, "So, where are you from?"

"New York. Mom and Dad divorced eight years ago. Mom moved here, but Dad stayed. It made sense for me to be with him until I finished high school. I traveled around a bit after, and now, I'm here."

"You transferred in, though, right?"

"Yes, it was my mother's idea. I was having a hard time, and she thought a change of scenery would be good for me."

Grinning, I ask, "So, do you like the scenery?"

Diandra laughs. "Well, it's getting better by the minute."

"Hey, Gray, you want drinks too?" yells Bruno.

"What would you like to drink?"

"Dr. Pepper if he's got it."

Standing, I jog the short distance to the van. Bruno holds out our food, and I take it off him, walking the dogs back to the table.

When I get back to him, he's grinning at me. "She's pretty, Gray."

"Her name is Diandra, and yeah, she is," I agree. "Hey, could I get a Dr. Pepper and a bottle of water, please?"

"Sure thing, bud."

Bruno is in his late fifties, skinny as a rake, and is always smiling. I hand him twenty dollars, and he gives me my change.

"Have a good night," he says with a wink.

"You too, old man."

"Hey, enough with the old shit!"

Laughing, I go back to Diandra, who's examining her meal.

"It tastes better than it looks, I promise."

"It looks amazing."

"And don't worry if you can't eat it all... I can always help you out."

Diandra's lips go up on one side of her mouth in a smirk. "Challenge accepted."

I bark out a laugh. "Woman, it wasn't meant to be a challenge. You're a tiny little thing. I just meant it's a big meal for someone your size."

"I haven't eaten since this morning. I've had a helluva day, and I'm starving. You just sit back and watch me eat it."

It's nice to be with a woman who isn't afraid to eat. My mom has never watched what she ate. Everything in moderation is her mantra. She doesn't own a car and rarely takes public transportation. Mom walks everywhere, so it's probably why she can afford to eat whatever she pleases.

Diandra takes a big bite, and sauce oozes down her face. I jump up and grab some napkins from the food truck. When I get back to her, she's trying to wipe her face with the back of her hand. Gratefully, she takes the napkins off me and tries to clean herself up.

After she's finished chewing, she says, "Thank you. I'm kind of a messy eater. I like to get involved in my food."

Laughing, I nod. "There's no easy way to eat one of these, and I like extra sauce, pickles, tomatoes, and onions, so you're bound to get messy."

"Good choices," replies Diandra, as she takes another bite, sending more sauce down her chin.

I don't laugh at her. I'm happy she likes the meal, and she doesn't even seem worried that dinner is a hotdog. Diandra looks out over the river and smiles. When she's finished chewing, she looks back at me. "It's a great spot. Thanks for bringing me here, Gray."

"You're not upset we didn't go to a party?"

"No, this is perfect. Does Bruno do dessert?"

"He might have some cream pie?"

"My treat." I shake my head, and she flutters a hand in front of my face. "No, really. Please let me." Diandra giggles. "Of course, it all depends if I can fit this in. Maybe we could share a dessert?"

"Let's see how we do?"

"Deal!"

CHAPTER 2

DIANDRA

The noise of the stadium is deafening as people chant for their teams. I'm sitting in the bleachers with Minerva Moore, Gray's mom.

"Is it always like this?" I ask.

Minerva smiles broadly at me. "No." She laughs. "It's normally louder." I chuckle, and she wraps an arm around me. "You'll get used to it."

Our college team runs onto the field, and the crowd roars.

Minerva points to her son. "There he is, number twenty-two. Doesn't his little butt look good in that uniform?"

"Minerva!" I shriek, laughing.

"Oh, hush. You two have been seeing each other for a month. I'm old, not dead. I remember what it was like."

My face heats up, and I stare out into the field. Gray and I haven't gone all the way yet. We're taking it slow. After my last encounter, I need to be sure he's not mentally unstable. Not that Gray is anything like Antony. He was way too possessive and needed to know where I was twenty-four hours a day. Gray gives me space, but it's early days.

The roar of the crowd brings me back to the present, and Minerva grabs my hand.

"Here we go!"

I know nothing about football. The only reason I've been to previous games was because a girl in one of my classes dragged me to them since she didn't want to go alone. She wanted to see the football players in their tight uniforms. As soon as I saw Gray, I was smitten.

Our first date was one of the best I've ever had. He was confident, funny, and that hotdog was one of the best I've ever had.

Minerva stands. "Go, Gray!"

Standing next to her, I try to find him on the field. It takes me a moment, his number twenty-two shining out like a beacon for me. Minerva sits, and I do too. She's bouncing up and down, acting like a much younger woman.

Her enthusiasm is catching.

Before long, we're at half-time, and Minerva is waving frantically at one of the hotdog vendors to get us something to eat and drink.

"Are hotdogs okay?"

"Minerva, let me get it."

She scowls at me and holds up two fingers to the man who comes right over.

"And two Dr. Pepper's," I say as I hand him a note. "Keep the change."

Minerva scowls at me. "It was my treat."

"You can get it next time."

She nods. "You enjoying the game?"

"Yes, it's great." Opening my Dr. Pepper, I take a sip and ask, "Are we winning?"

Minerva slaps my thigh. "Yes, we're winning!" Her laugher is infectious. "He's blitzed the pass three times. My boy is on fire," she proudly boasts.

It's obvious I need to do some research on football before the next game, as I have no clue what Minerva is talking about.

"Has he always wanted to play?"

Minerva takes a bite of her hotdog and nods. "Yeah, Gray's a natural." She smiles. "It won't be long before he gets the attention from one of the scouts for the pros."

"What will that mean?"

"It'll mean he'll make enough money to do whatever he wants. Gray knows that football is a young man's game, and he could easily get hurt. Has he told you about his five-year plan?" I shake my head. "Well, he will. I'll leave that to him. He's focused, eyes on the prize."

"He's studying sports medicine, isn't he?"

"Yes." Minerva smiles. "I told him he had to have a backup plan. Sometimes life throws you a curveball, and you have to adapt."

I laugh. "Did you just use a baseball term for a football player?"

Minerva chuckles. "Yes, I did."

The whistle sounds, and all conversation stops. I'm grateful I get to eat my hotdog and watch Gray on the field. Minerva is a good mom. From the little Gray has told me, his dad died when he was five, and his mom never remarried or even dated. She made it her mission to provide for her son and make sure he went to college. Getting a scholarship took the financial burden off her, but she still takes care of him. Her dedication is to be admired.

Gray loves his mom. It's evident in the way he talks and treats her. It's just been the two of them for a long time now.

I'm waiting with Minerva for Gray to come out of the locker room. We won, so the atmosphere is electric. A bunch of people are waiting outside, mostly family and friends, but there's also a quite a large female group. Their hair and makeup are a little overdone for a football game, and one of them is looking at me with open hostility. I shift nervously, and Minerva catches me trying to smooth my hair.

"Oh, don't fuss. That one is Lisa. She and Gray dated for a minute. She's looking for a payday." Minerva puts an arm around me. "You look beautiful. Unlike some, you don't need to plaster on the makeup, your beauty shines from within."

Her words make me feel instantly better, although part of me wishes my hair was smoother. Gray walks out, and Lisa throws her arms around him. He smiles down at her as she kisses his cheek. Gray glances at me, his smile falters at whatever he can see on my face. The way I'm feeling, I bet it's a shade of green from jealousy, and then he tries to disentangle himself from her.

Without thinking, I march up to them and push in between the two of them. Then, I put my arms around Gray's neck and kiss him on the lips.

"Congratulations, baby!" I kiss him again. "Come on, your mom is waiting." With my hand firmly grasping his, I drag him toward Minerva.

Minerva is laughing. I let Gray go so he can hug his mother.

"You did good, son." Minerva is beaming up at him. "Let's go get something to eat."

Gray smiles down at her. "I'm starving."

"You always are." Minerva winks up at him.

Gray holds out a hand to each of us, and we leave the stadium. When we get to his car, he opens the doors for us to climb in. I get in the back so Minerva can sit comfortably in the front. Gray is outside the car talking to a couple of his teammates.

Minerva twists in her seat. "You okay, honey?"

My face heats in embarrassment. "*Lisa* annoyed me."

Minerva nods. "There's a lot of Lisa's out there, honey. Don't let them get to you. Gray looks at you like you set the moon in the night sky. He never looked at Lisa that way, and he never invited Lisa to sit with me in the bleachers. You're the first."

"Really?" Minerva nods. "I got angry."

Minerva chuckles. "Oh, honey, I saw that. And maybe it was a good thing. Lisa might leave him alone now. I swear that girl has no class."

Minerva twists back around in her seat as Gray slides in.

"Where do my two favorite ladies want to go?"

"Gray, you normally eat pizza after a game," states Minerva.

"I know, Mom, just thought you and Dee might like something else?"

"Pizza works for me," I say, and Minerva nods.

"Pizza it is!" replies Gray with a hand raised in the air like he's won a victory.

We're sitting outside my apartment in Gray's car. We dropped Minerva off at her apartment. It's just the two of us, but the silence feels stifling. Glancing at him, I find he's staring at me.

"Do you want to come in?" I ask.

Gray shakes his head. I smile at him and reach for the door handle.

"Dee?"

I twist in the seat. "Yeah?"

Gray turns and stares out the windshield, then he shakes his head. "Maybe, I'll come in for a minute."

Confused, I open my door. "Okay."

I get out, and Gray is already jogging toward my apartment building so he can open the door for me. I unlock the door, and he waves me in.

"You know I can open the door," I tease.

"I know."

His silence and seriousness have me on edge. I keep walking toward my apartment, open the door, and head for the kitchen.

"You want a coffee?"

"No."

"Cold drink?"

"No."

I stop what I'm doing and stare at him. "What do you want, Gray?"

He takes my hand and leads me to the couch, where he sits down and pulls me with him. "Can we talk about tonight?"

"Sure? What about it?"

Gray keeps my hand firmly in his grasp while his other hand rests on my knee, then he looks me in the eyes. "Lisa doesn't mean anything."

His words seem to strike at something deep within me, and I try to pull away from him, anger and embarrassment rising inside of me. Gray's hands go to my shoulders, forcing me to look at him.

"After every game, there's always a bunch of them hanging around. At first, I was flattered. I went from Mr. Nobody to the guy they wanted to know." He shakes his head. "But they don't know me. Girls like Lisa see a way out of their situation. I've got to admit, it took me a minute to catch on to her plan, but my mom was wise to it all along."

I narrow my gaze, and my lips turn down. "You seemed to like the attention."

Gray shakes his head. "You're worth a million Lisa's or whatever their names are. Babe, you know *me*. You know my mom. *I want you*."

His words melt my heart, and I close the gap between us, my lips crashing into his. Gray growls and lifts me, so I'm straddling him on the couch. The kiss goes from passionate to a wild frenzy in a heartbeat. Suddenly, I have too many clothes on, and my body feels like it's on fire. Gray puts his hands under my ass and stands, and my legs instantly wrap around him. He keeps walking, and the next thing I know, we're in my bedroom, and he's laying me down on the bed. I kick off my shoes, then Gray's hands go under my sweater and lift it. His fingers grope at my bra, pulling it down on one side, then his lips leave mine to lock onto my hardened nipple—an electric feeling pulses through me.

"Gray!" I gasp as I hold his head in place.

His hand pulls down my bra on the other side, and he moves to the other nipple. The warmth of his mouth on me causes another moan to escape. Gray's hand moves down my body, trailing fire along my side. He keeps going down my leg and then to my inner thigh. Finally, his hand applies pressure to my pussy through my jeans, and it's nearly too much.

Reaching down, I pull my sweater up and over my head and remove my bra. Gray lays kisses down my stomach, his hands go to my belt, and he undoes it. Next, he tugs at the button and zipper. His hands pull my jeans down, and when he gets to my knees, he stops. I cry out in frustration, and he smiles. Gray bends and buries his face between my legs, lapping at me through the thin lacy material of my panties.

"Gray!"

I hold his head in place as his tongue works me into a frenzy. Unashamedly, I grind into his face, holding him steady as my body shatters into a million pieces. The orgasm hits me so hard, it takes my breath away.

Gray keeps going until he elicits every last aftershock out of me, then slowly, he pulls my panties and jeans off me.

"Beautiful," he whispers, staring down at my naked body.

Deliberately, he removes all of his clothing. Even in the dim light of my bedroom, I can see his well-defined body, sculpted from endless hours at the gym. My eyes trace his six-pack, which goes down into a 'V.' He's the beautiful one. Gray is perfect, his cock is twelve inches of rock-hard goodness that glistens in the light.

Sitting, I take the tip into my mouth. Gray groans, his hands entangling themselves in my hair as he gently rocks into my eager mouth. I swirl my tongue across the tip, and he hisses in appreciation.

Gray pulls out of my mouth and pushes me back onto the bed. I watch as he opens his wallet and puts a condom on his enlarged cock. He covers my body with his, his cock teasing me at my entrance.

I slip one leg and then the other around him, giving him unfettered access to my body. His cocks slides in between my folds, but he doesn't enter me. Gray rolls us, so I'm on top, and as I straighten up, he slides me onto him. I gasp at the intrusion inside me. His hands move to my hips as he moves me, arching up inside me as he does. The position hits my G-spot, and I cry out. "Oh, my God!"

"Not quite, honey, but let's see if we can get you to heaven."

I roll my hips, and he arches up again, evoking the same response.

"Don't stop," I whimper.

Gray keeps thrusting inside me as I grind onto him faster and faster. My body feels like it's melting and my feet are burning. The orgasm sweeps through me. Unlike ones I've had before, it keeps building like a tidal wave.

"Gray!" The voice doesn't sound like me—it's a cross between a scream and an animalist growl.

The orgasm feels like it's never going to end, and my body is molten lava. Gray flips us and pumps into me harder. His thumb goes to my nub, applying pressure, and I swear the tidal wave turns into a tsunami as wave after wave of pleasure rocks through me.

A growl escapes Gray as he finds his release, and still, I'm riding his cock as my body shudders for the last time, milking him of his seed and taking all of him.

"My feet were on fire," I whisper.

Gray chuckles. "That's a first."

"You can say that again."

Gray lowers himself onto me and kisses me lightly. "Like a sword in a scabbard, you fit me perfectly."

I giggle. "A sword in a scabbard?"

Gray rises and nods. "Yep."

My hands go to his handsome face, cupping it. "You couldn't come up with a better analogy?"

Gray kisses my nose. "Nope."

Smiling, I nod. "Okay, baby. A sword it is."

Gray smiles and slowly pulls out of me. "I'll be back."

The loss of his cock and body is instant. I don't like it. Gray pads into my bathroom, and I'm glad one of us had the presence of mind to use a condom. Slowly, I stand on shaking legs, waiting for him to do what he needs to do. When he comes out, I go in and tidy myself up. Gray is lying in my bed with the covers over himself. As I enter the room, he pulls down one side, and I climb in next to him.

"Is it okay if I stay?"

So like Gray, always making sure I'm okay.

"I'd be mad if you didn't."

I tuck myself into his side, placing one leg over his.

"This feels good."

"Yeah, it does," I agree.

My hand travels down his stomach over his abs and back up. Before sleep takes me, my last thought is how lucky I am that Gray and I fit like a sword in a scabbard, and I smile at his silly comparison.

CHAPTER 3

DIANDRA

Gray is the most amazing man. Tonight we're going to a party organized by his best friend, Colton Anders. Colt is also on the football team. He looks like the All-American, and women fall at his feet. Not only is he good-looking, but Colt has a silver tongue with the ladies. When we first met, Gray told me he told him to back off. Not that Colt would've tried anything—it's obvious he adores Gray and his mom and wouldn't do anything to jeopardize their friendship.

A knock at my door has me hurrying to open it, even though I'm only in a towel. I glance at the clock, and Gray is forty minutes early.

Throwing open the door, I'm shocked to see Anton standing there.

"Hello, Diandra."

I slam the door shut and lock it. My cell phone is in the kitchen, and I run to it and dial Gray.

"Hey, baby," he says cheerfully. "Miss me?"

"Gray," I cry. "How far away are you?"

Anton pounds on my door.

"What's wrong?"

"There's someone here, and I need him to leave. It's a long story." The pounding on my door intensifies, and I let out a squeal.

"I'm on my way but ring the police." Gray ends the call, and I dial 9-1-1.

"This is 9-1-1, what's your emergency?"

"A man trying to get into my apartment. I have a restraining order against him in Texas. Does that apply here?"

"We have a police vehicle en route. What's your name?"

"Diandra Evergrow. His name is Anton Burr. He stalked me in Texas."

"Is he in your apartment?"

"No, ma'am." I hear sirens outside my window. "I think the police are here."

"Don't leave your apartment. Stay on the line."

Quickly, I move into my bedroom and put on a robe. There's a knock at my door, and I freeze in motion until I hear, "Boston, police, Ms. Evergrow."

This time I look through the peephole before I open the door. Out in the hallway are two policemen and no sign of Anton. I unlock the door and let them in.

"He was here only a moment ago." Looking out into the hallway, no one else is around. Quickly, I close the door and follow the police into my living room.

One police officer does a quick sweep of my apartment. "Ma'am, you told the 9-1-1 operator that you have a restraining order against this individual?"

"Yes, his name is Anton Burr. It was filed in Texas."

"It's enforceable here in Boston."

Relieved, I nod furiously. "I moved here to get away from him."

There's a knock on my door, followed by, "Dee! Are you okay?"

A police officer moves toward the door.

"It's my boyfriend, Grayson Moore."

"Grayson Moore of the Eagles?"

Smiling, I nod. He opens the door, and Gray steps back.

"Officer, my girlfriend, Diandra Evergrow, lives here. Is she okay?"

The officer moves out of the way and says, "Yes, she's fine. The offender fled before we arrived."

Gray walks past the officer and straight to me. "Are you okay?"

"I'm fine. Anton didn't do anything. He gave me a scare. I was expecting you, not him."

One of the officers clears his throat, and we both stare at him. "We'll do a sweep of the neighborhood. In the meantime, you take care and call us if he shows up again. Don't take any chances."

"Thank you so much, officers. I appreciate how quickly you got here."

"We were in the neighborhood." The officer's attention goes from me to Gray. "Great game last night. You boys are playing well."

Gray smiles and shakes the officer's hand. "You follow the Eagles?"

"Yeah, I played in my younger days."

The officer nods at me, then Gray, and then he and his partner leave. Gray follows them to the door, locks it, and hurries back to me. "What happened?"

Wrapping my arms around myself, I sit on the couch. Gray joins me, putting a protective arm around me.

"Back in Texas, I dated a guy. At first, he was very sweet, but he changed. Anton wanted to know where I was every second of every day. When I tried to break it off, he became aggressive. He followed me everywhere. Then one day, he was waiting for me in my dorm room."

"Did he hurt you?"

I shake my head. "Scared me pretty good. He's the reason I moved here. Anton stuck to the restraining order and was always the required distance away, but he'd push the limits. If I went to the grocery store and he was there, he'd say it was a coincidence. It got so I was scared to leave my dorm."

"But he never hurt you?"

"No."

Gray looks relieved. "What do you want to do?"

"He scares me, Gray."

"I won't let him anywhere near you. I'll stay here, and if I can't be here, you can stay with my mom. She loves you, so it won't be an issue."

Leaning forward, I rest my head on his arm. "Thank you."

"Do you still want to go to Colt's party?"

I nod. "Anton stole six months of my life, and he's not getting anymore."

Gray smiles. "That's my girl."

The party is in full swing. The music is loud, and half a dozen girls surround Colt, all vying for his attention. You can tell he's not serious about any of them. He and Gray were going to play beer pong, but because of Anton, they both decided not to drink so they chose teams. The losing team has to drink. So far, Gray is winning, which is making Colt unhappy.

"You're cheating," states Colt.

"How am I cheating? Come on, Mr. Quarterback, can't you throw?"

"Fuck you."

"You talk to my momma with that mouth?"

"Your momma loves me."

Gray laughs and nods. "But not as much as me."

Colt nods. "I still think you're cheating."

Shaking my head at their antics, I walk upstairs to the bathroom. The line is ten people deep. With a groan, I go back downstairs. Colt and Gray are still playing beer pong so I walk outside.

Not long later a hand lands on my shoulder, and I shriek in fright. It's Gray.

"Where are you going?"

"I need to go to the bathroom, and the line is long, so I thought I'd go to the gas station."

"Not without me." Gray puts his hand in mine, and we walk along the sidewalk.

"Colt must be upset that you stopped the game."

"He's claiming victory, telling everyone I forfeited." Gray laughs and shakes his head. "Colt doesn't like to lose."

We walk hand in hand until we get to the gas station. Walking inside, I grab a candy bar and put it on the counter.

"Could I have the key to the restrooms, please?"

"You gotta buy something."

I point at the candy bar. The young guy harrumps, reaches under the counter, and gives me a key attached to a large wooden spoon.

"Bring back the key," he orders.

I smile sweetly at him and hurry to the bathroom. Going into the cubicle, I do what I need to do, then open the door to come out and wash my hands. It has one of those automatic taps where you wave your hand and the water flows. A door behind me opens, catching my eye. I turn, thinking it's going to be another woman, but Anton walks out.

"Gray!" I scream as loud as I can.

"Calm down, Diandra. I don't want to hurt you."

Running for the door, I open it. "Gray!"

Anton slams the door shut. "I only want to talk to you."

"Keep away from me!"

"Don't be like that, Diandra. I've missed you. Please, talk to me."

"Gray!"

"Who the fuck is Gray?" demands Anton.

The door to the ladies bursts open, and Gray tackles Anton to the floor.

"I'm Gray, motherfucker, and that's my girl you're scaring."

Gray sits on his back and twists Anton's arm up behind his back.

"You're hurting me!" cries Anton like a child.

"Dee, are you okay?"

"Y-Yes!"

"Call 9-1-1."

Anton tries to squirm out of Gray's grip, but it's to no avail. My man has him firmly pinned down. Pulling my cell phone out of my pocket, I'm about to dial the police when an officer opens the bathroom door.

"What the hell is going on here?" The officer has his gun drawn.

With my hands up, I say, "Officer, this man attacked me, and I have a restraining order against him."

The officer looks from me to the two men on the floor. Another officer joins us in the small bathroom.

"What the hell is going on?"

"Sir, this man attacked my girlfriend. She has a restraining order against him."

The second officer puts his hand on the other officer's gun, pushing it down, and steps further into the room.

"You're Grayson Moore, linebacker for the Eagles, aren't you?"

"Yes, sir."

The policeman nods and glances at his partner, who puts his gun away.

"Son, you need to get off him so we can do our job."

"I haven't done anything!" yells Anton.

Gray pushes his head into the tiled floor before he climbs off him, then walks to me, enveloping me in a hug. "Are you okay?"

I nod.

One of the officers puts handcuffs on Anton and pulls him to his feet.

Anton looks at Gray and me and yells, "Don't touch her, she's mine!"

The officers drag Anton out of the bathroom as he hurls insults and profanities at Gray and me. Shaking in fear, Gray holds me tighter, and we walk out of the gas station to a sea of blue flashing lights as two more police cruisers pull into the gas station.

Anton is screaming as they force him into the back of one of the cars. The first officer on the scene comes toward me.

"Ma'am, we're going to need you both to come down to the station and make a statement."

I nod, and he escorts us to another police car.

Hours later, back at my apartment, Gray holds me close in the darkness. Anton was taken into custody, and the arresting officer seemed to think he'd end up in a psych ward instead of a cell. He screamed nonstop about how I was his. Either way, Anton's out of my life for good.

"Are you okay?"

"You saved me."

"I should never have let you go into that bathroom alone. I watched him walk in after you, but he seemed normal, then I heard you scream." Gray kisses my temple. "I've never been so scared, Dee. The thought of him hurting you…"

"He didn't hurt me, and he'll never have the opportunity to again."

Gray kisses me once more and holds me tighter. Safe in his arms, I fall asleep.

CHAPTER 4

GRAYSON

The football season is over. Dee and I have been together for over a year, and I am now in negotiations with the New England Warriors. I haven't told Diandra as I want it to be a surprise. The Warriors aren't the only team looking at me, but they have a new owner, he's young, and his name is Tyson Reed. He made his money in computer software. The guy was a billionaire by the time he turned thirty. Tyson has a vision for the team, his eyes firmly set on the Super Bowl. He's also offering me the most money.

I'm a linebacker, and the highest-paid linebacker in the league is earning nine million dollars. I'm younger, keener, and have a longer life in pro-ball ahead of me. Right now, there's talk of a seven-million-dollar deal. It's good, but I'm hoping to do better. And besides, I've got one more year of college ball. This way I can prove myself to the scouts and maybe pick up a good agent. If I keep going the way I am, a multi-million-dollar deal will set me, my mom, and hopefully, Diandra up for the rest of our lives.

I can see myself settling down with Dee. The only thing standing in our way is her reaction to the fans. Strike that, the *female* fans. It doesn't matter how many times I tell her I'm just being nice, she still gets angry. Mom thinks it's funny, but I don't understand how she can even think I'd be into anyone besides her.

Dee is smart, beautiful, and it makes my day to hear her voice. No other woman compares. Her jealousy is ridiculous. I'm looking forward to spending time with Dee away from the field and fans, and it only being about us.

She's been working hard at the accounting firm, getting practical experience. The way she talks about her boss, it sounds as though he'll want her to work for him at their New York agency when she graduates.

"Gray!"

Turning, I see Dee running toward me. Holding out my arms, she runs right into them.

"Hey, beautiful."

She kisses my lips quickly. "What are you doing here?"

"I've got time off for good behavior, so I thought I'd come find you."

Dee giggles. I'm cutting training today. Even though the season is over, we still train. Coach will give me hell for it, but I wanted to spend some quality time with her. She flattens her hands on my chest and looks up at me, and I'm blown away at how lucky I am.

"I can't, babe. My boss has a big client coming in, and I said I'd help. This girl's gotta work." I frown at her. "You understand, don't you?"

"Yeah, yeah, I do. Maybe this weekend we could do something?"

Dee shakes her head. "I'm working all weekend, and I need to study."

"What about dinner? You have to eat, right?"

Dee smiles. "My boss, James, was going to order in for us."

"James?"

"Mr. Brookes."

"You call your boss James now?"

Her hands drop to her sides. "Sometimes. We all do."

I puff out my cheeks. "Okay."

"Don't be like that, Gray. I never complain when you have to train."

She's right, she doesn't. I know this job is important to her, and it's a stepping stone to bigger and better things, much like me and college ball.

"Sorry. I miss you, is all."

"Next weekend? I'll make sure to clear my schedule," Dee teases.

Smiling down at her, I shake my head. "Can't next weekend. I've got a meet and greet with some of the pro leagues. Coach set it up."

Dee bounces up and down. "Do you think you'll get signed?"

"Not this year, but maybe for next. I've been playing well, and I'm one of the most well-rounded players on the team. My stats are looking pretty good, especially my missed tackles are at an all-time low of five point one percent. No else comes close."

Dee's eyes glaze over slightly as I talk statistics. She's tried hard to grasp aspects of the game, and for the most part, Dee gets it, but I guess it can get a little monotonous hearing me discuss stats off the top of my head.

Dee grabs my shirt with both hands and pulls me in for a kiss. "You're going to do great, Gray. I just know it. The sky's the limit for you."

"For us."

Dee smiles. "For us."

CHAPTER 5

DIANDRA

I'm bending over a desk, making sure I've got all the paperwork in the correct piles for my boss, James Brookes. He has a client coming in tonight from out of town, and I know he wants to land him. It'll be a big contract for the firm.

You know that feeling when you can sense someone is watching you? I turn and find my boss staring at me with his cell phone to his ear. He nods at me and smiles, then quickly ends the call.

"We all set?"

I smile at him. "Yes, sir." There's a mountain of paperwork on the desk, but I think I've got everything he needs. "You're all set. We just need the client to arrive."

"You've done great work on this, Diandra. In fact, you've done great work for us ever since you started here." James moves in closer. "Have you thought more about our offer?"

At the end of the year, I'll have completed my accounting degree—four years of hard work. Mr. Brookes' firm has a branch in New York, and he thinks I'd be a good fit. It's something I want to do, but it would mean leaving Gray, and the very thought of doing that causes my heart to ache.

I shake my head slightly.

James puts his hands on my shoulders. "Don't let some boy ruin what could be a very good career. You don't want just to be a football player's wife, do you?"

I shake my head. "No, but there has to be a way to have it all. I just haven't figured out how yet."

The sound of someone clearing their throat draws both of our attentions. Standing at the door is Gray.

James drops his hands and walks to him, his hand extended. "Gray, good to see you."

"Yeah," replies Gray with a frown.

"I was telling your girl here that we need someone like her in New York."

"Oh, really?" says Gray, his eyes coming to me.

I smile. "Mr. Brookes is just being nice."

James laughs. "I am many things, but I'm not nice unless I can get something out of it, and Gray..." he turns to him, "... I want her in New York. Talk Diandra into it. She's an asset to our team, and when she graduates, she'll walk straight into a high-paying position in one of the most exciting cities in the country." James walks out of the room, leaving me alone with Gray.

He's still frowning as he walks closer to me. "What was that?"

"James offered me a job. I haven't said yes. I wanted to talk to you about it."

"No, not that. Why did he have his hands on you?"

Now it's my turn to frown. "What?"

"When I walked in, he had his hands on you. Is there something you need to tell me, Dee?"

I scoff. "Don't be ridiculous. He's fifteen years older than me and married!"

"Did he or did he not just have his hands on you?"

Shaking my head, I walk toward Gray. "It was nothing!"

"Right."

"I have to put up with fans fawning all over you, and you're jealous that my boss, my older boss, was trying to convince me to move to New York? And the only reason I'm not saying yes is because of *you*."

Gray takes a step back. "What do you mean?"

"Gray, I love you. Leaving you isn't something I want to do. I love us, and I'm excited about the life we're going to live *together*."

Gray's arms surround me in a hug. "I'm sorry. It's the same for me. I guess I went a little crazy just now. Maybe I finally understand how you feel when you see me with other women? They mean nothing, they're fans, but seeing you with Mr. Brookes, I could've beaten him to a pulp."

I squeeze him tighter and laugh. "James is a good man and devoted to his wife."

"Good to know." For a moment, Gray is silent, and then he asks, "Is it something you want? To move to New York?"

"It's a tremendous opportunity, but there will be others. I don't need to decide right now." Pulling back from Gray, I gaze into his kind eyes. "I'm hoping he offers me a position here."

"Why here?"

"Well, if you get signed by the New England Warriors, it'll mean you'll stay here. It makes sense, doesn't it?"

Gray takes my hands in his. "You'd give up New York for me?"

"I'd give up everything for you, Gray. We're a team."

Gray presses his lips to my forehead. "Yes, we are."

CHAPTER 6

GRAYSON

Twelve Months Later

"Hey, Mom!" I yell as I enter her apartment.

"Gray?"

I find her in the kitchen, apron on, cooking fried chicken. Bending, I kiss her cheek and then take a leg off the plate.

"These are for later," Mom admonishes with a shake of her head.

I take a bite of the crispy seasoned chicken that's better than anything store-bought. "So good!"

Mom smiles. "How's Diandra?"

I smile back at her. "Good."

"You two have been dating for a while now."

"Yeah, it'll be a year soon."

"Her mom told me she got offered a job in New York?"

"Yeah, her boss wants her to go, but Dee wants to stay with me."

"Sounds like it's a wonderful opportunity for her."

"Mom, I'm going to finish out this season. If I get signed, Diandra won't need to work then. I'll be making enough for all of us."

Mom puts down her tongs. "Oh, Gray. It's not about the money. Diandra doesn't care about that. She wants more for herself, you understand, don't you?"

Frowning, I put down the chicken. "What do you mean?"

"She's studied for four years, Gray. It's like you and football. You love it, and it's your dream. Well, Diandra's dream is to work in her chosen field."

It never occurred to me to look at it that way. Mom is right. Diandra has studied and worked hard to achieve her goals, just like I have. She'd never be happy just being my wife.

"What do I do?"

Mom smiles. "Talk to her. Tell her about your five-year plan. Ask her what hers is, and then go from there. I think you two are destined for one another, but all relationships take work, and it can't all be one-sided."

Picking up the leg, I finish it, then wipe my mouth on the back of my hand. Mom throws a dish towel, hitting me in the face. "Don't do that." She shakes her head. "You want some more?"

"Yes, please."

Mom smiles and pulls a plate off the top shelf, then places two pieces of chicken on it. I eat it in silence, thinking over what she's said. It's selfish of me to think that Diandra isn't as focused as I am. She works just as hard.

"You seem a thousand miles away."

"I think it's time Dee and I talk, especially with what's coming soon."

Mom stops what she's doing, a smile of approval on her face. "You've been approached?"

"Yes, ma'am, by more than one."

"Did you get the one you wanted?"

Mom is standing in front of me now, shifting from foot to foot, excitement exuding from her very being.

"The New England Warriors want me."

Mom throws her arms around me. "I'm so proud of you!"

"I haven't signed with anyone... yet."

"No, but you will." Mom kisses my cheek and moves back. "Now, eat. Then go find that girl of yours and tell her the good news."

"Ahh, mom?"

"Yes, honey?"

"Can we keep this between us for now?"

"You're not going to tell her?"

"I will, but not till the deal is signed, and I *know* where I'm going."

Diandra is walking out of work, and I honk the horn to gain her attention. She looks up and waves, hurrying toward the car.

"I wasn't expecting to see you today." Her gorgeous face lights up with a smile.

"Thought I'd surprise you. You hungry?"

"Yeah."

"Hotdogs?"

"Down by the river?"

"Would we go anywhere else?"

Dee laughs. "Well, a guy once told me they are the best in the city."

We drive in companionable silence on the short drive. It takes me back to our first date, except the sun hasn't set. We both get out of the car and walk hand in hand to the food truck.

"Hey, Gray and Dee, you want the usual?" yells Bruno when he sees us.

"Yes, please!" yells back Dee and sits at our table.

I sit opposite her and hold out my hands to her. She immediately puts hers in mine.

"You okay? You seem preoccupied."

I smile and run my thumb across her knuckles. "I've got big plans for next year, and I was talking to Mom about them, and she asked me what your goals were. It occurred to me we haven't talked about long-term plans for us."

"Grayson!" yells out Colt from about twenty feet away.

I wave, and he lumbers over with a new girl on his arm. Colt has blond hair, blue eyes, muscles, and is tall. The women fall all over him. My mom calls him trouble, but I know she loves him.

Colt sits down at the table next to me, and his latest sits next to Diandra.

"Can we join you?" he asks.

"I think you already have," I tease.

"You want something to eat?" he asks his date.

"Do they have anything low carb or vegetarian?" she asks.

Leaning over the table, I hold out my hand. "Hi, I'm Grayson, and this is Diandra."

She takes my hand. "I'm Cindy."

"How'd you two meet?" asks Diandra.

"It's the cutest story! Colt was jogging past, I was doing yoga in the park, and he tripped."

"She was doing downward dog," replies Colt with a grin.

Diandra laughs. "Love at first sight."

"Come on, babe, let's see if Bruno has something you'll eat."

I watch them walk away. "He's hopeless." I look back at Dee, who's shaking her head. "Do you mind that they're joining us?"

"No, not at all. You hardly spend any time with him."

"That's not true. I see him just about every day."

"Training and football don't count. When was the last time you two hung out?"

I groan. "Colt likes to party. He attracts too much attention."

"Well, he *is* the quarterback."

"He's a show-off, always has been. And the way his family is, I don't blame him."

"They aren't close?"

"No. And with girls, he always takes the easy path. God help the woman who finally says no to him 'cause he won't know what to do."

Colt comes back and slaps me on the back. "Bruno says your order is up."

"Where's Cindy?" I ask as I stand.

"She doesn't eat anything that Bruno has for sale, so we're catching up later."

"Oh, no, trouble in paradise?" teases Diandra.

Colt sits down and shakes his head. "Nope, just a bump in the road."

"How long is that road? One day or two?" quips Diandra.

Colt blushes. "More like hours."

I laugh. "Be nice to *my* girl."

"He's always nice, Gray. Can you get me a water, too, please?"

"Sure. Colt, you want anything?"

"Nah, I've ordered. Although, if your girl ever gets tired of you..." He waggles his eyebrows up and down.

"Don't even joke about shit like that." I punch him lightly on the arm and walk over to Bruno.

"Good to see, ya, Gray!" booms Bruno. "How are things looking for you this year? I saw your last game. The quarterback over there did good, but I kept my eye on you. You did better."

"Yeah, the quarterback gets all the glory." Bruno hands me our hotdogs, and I slide a twenty toward him. "Can I get two waters, too, please?"

Bruno turns and grabs them, then leans down and says softly, "Colt is an outstanding player, but he's not as disciplined as you. Hell, just look at all the different girls he's had in the past two years. I've given up on trying to remember their names."

I chuckle. "Yeah, the ladies love Colt."

Bruno is wrong about Colt and football—it's all he has. If he's not training or playing, he's at my mom's place. She calls him the son from another mother, the child she never gave birth to but has claimed. Colt comes across as a carefree playboy, and the playboy part might be true, but like for me, football is his ticket to a better life.

Walking back to them, they are deep in conversation. Diandra is leaning toward Colt, listening intently to whatever it is he's saying.

I sit next to Colt, and the conversation stops.

Diandra looks at me, a small frown on her forehead.

"What did I miss?"

"You're in talks with the New England Warriors?"

I purse my lips at Colt, then stare at Diandra.

"I was going to tell you. It's why I brought you here, so we could talk."

"Sorry, man, didn't know it was a secret."

I slide a hotdog over to Dee. "It's not. I just hadn't got around to telling Dee yet."

Colt looks sheepish and rubs the back of his neck. "Did I ruin a surprise?"

Dee reaches over and pats Colt's hand. "No. I knew the scouts and the league were sniffing around." She looks at me. "And you did say this was going to be your last year of college ball."

"Yep." Colt slaps me on the back. "Gray is on track for his five-year plan, and everything is working out, just like he thought it would."

Internally, I groan. Outwardly, I shake my head slightly at him. "If you fail to plan, you plan to fail."

Colt leans across the table. "If it weren't for Gray and his mom, I'd be a failure. They taught me you have to have a plan, and you have to stick to it."

Dee smiles at him. "What's your plan, Colt?"

"Like Gray, I'm going into professional ball next year. I've finally settled on an agent." Colt stares at me. "You should check him out, his name is Tom Fellow. Seems like a good guy, a straight-shooter."

"Yeah, I've spoken to him. He seems competent, but I was thinking of going with the same agent who represents Jamal McHenry."

Colt's eyes widen. Jamal McHenry is the highest-paid linebacker in the league. He has endorsements for a bunch of sports companies and even a deal with Calvin Klein.

"That's amazing, Gray!" Colt beams at me.

Throughout our conversation, Dee remains quiet. I smile at her, and she smiles back as she picks up her hotdog and takes a bite. Sauce and onion fall out, covering her chin with them. I hold up a napkin, which she takes off me as she nods her head.

"You know, Dee, you're the only girl I know who eats these," says Colt. "All the girls I bring here either don't eat meat, or they order the smallest thing on the menu, or worse, they only order water."

Dee finishes her mouthful. "You're dating the wrong women."

"Yo, Colt! Order's up!" yells Bruno.

Colt bounds away, leaving me alone with Dee.

"Babe, I was going to tell you about the New England Warriors tonight and ask you what your goals are. It's not something we've talked about."

"I've always known your plan was to go pro."

"Yeah, but like Colt said, I've got a five-year plan. It's all about to come together, and I want you to be a part of that."

Dee gives me a hard smile. "You want me to be a part of your plan? Was I always part of the plan? Or was it more like insert female here?"

Holding up my hands, I wave them in front of her. "No, no, no! Nothing like that." Reaching out across the table, I grab one of her hands. "You have to know what you mean to me. I love you, Dee."

Her face softens, and the smile becomes genuine.

Colt flops down beside me, dropping some of his food on our hands. "Sorry!" He stuffs one end of the hot dog into his mouth and takes a huge bite. "So good." Food nearly falls out of his mouth, but he pushes it back in.

Dee wipes the food off her hand, then mine as she shakes her head at Colt.

"Man, my momma would whoop your ass for eating like that," I berate him.

"What?" he asks again with a mouthful of food, then laughs. "Sorry, man."

I quirk an eyebrow at him. "I'm going to tell Mom what a mess you are."

"No fair!" Colt puts down his hotdog. "Your mom loves me. She won't believe you."

"She will if I back him up," replies Dee with a smirk.

"Oh, I see... I see how this is going. Just gang up on poor old Colt." He points at both of us. "You should be ashamed." Colt makes a big deal of shaking his head and trying to look hurt.

Dee and I exchange a glance, then burst out laughing. I shove Colt, who grins and picks up his hotdog. It makes me happy that my best friend and my girl get along so well. It cements in my mind that Dee is the woman for me.

We're back at Dee's place, and she's been quiet since we got in the car. She's in her small kitchen, fussing with the coffee machine.

Walking up behind her, I place my hands on her shoulders and kiss her neck. "Are you okay?"

"What's your five-year plan?" The words are almost a whisper, as though she's scared to find out.

"I guess it's more like a life plan." Turning her around, I put her hand in mine and pull her toward the couch. Dee sits next to me, nestling into my side. Draping an arm around her, I play with a lock of her hair between my fingers. "The plan, so far, is to win a college football scholarship and get signed, hopefully with the New England Warriors."

Dee shifts and looks up at me. "So far, it's all working out for you."

"Almost. I'm not signed yet."

"What else?"

"Get a deal. A good deal. Finish my degree, win the Super Bowl and go into private practice when I can't play anymore."

"That's it?" Her lips are turned down.

"No. I'll stop all of it if you don't want me to. If you don't see yourself in my future, in my plan, I'll change it." I cup the side of her face with one of my hands. "What do you want?"

Dee sits up and turns to face me. "I want to finish my degree. I've always wanted to have my own agency. Working for Mr. Brookes has shown me I'm more than capable." Dee's eyes land on my chest. "Later, I'd hoped I would get married, have children, and live happily ever after."

"Insert man here?" I tease.

Dee stands, wraps her arms around herself, and gives me her back. "Don't tease."

Standing, I place my arms around her. "I'm not. Not really."

Reaching up, I sweep her hair off her shoulder, exposing the side of her neck. I place kisses there, causing her to shiver. Dee twists in my arms, her lips crashing onto mine.

"I love you, Grayson Moore."

Pulling back, I smile at her. "Ahh, we've found one thing we can agree on. We love each other."

Walking her backward, I smile down at her as she allows me to manhandle her toward the bedroom. Dee's hands move to my belt, and she has it undone and my zipper down with her hand stroking my cock as we walk through the doorway.

"Woman, the things you do to me."

"I could stop?"

Sucking my bottom lip in between my teeth, I shake my head. "Don't you dare."

Dee sits on the bed, and my jeans and underwear hit the floor with a loud thud. Her mouth lowers onto my cock, and my fingers immerse themselves in her hair, guiding her up and down. One of Dee's hands cups my balls, and I growl in appreciation.

The familiar tingle hits my balls, and I know I'm close. With a groan, I pull away from her and push her back onto the bed. My only thought is that I want to bury myself inside her. Roughly, I remove her panties and push up her skirt. Dee opens her legs, and I ease myself into her tight, wet pussy. Dee gasps, her nails digging into my arms. Embedded inside of her, I place her legs on either side of my head and then slowly withdraw my cock. Dee smiles up at me, and I slam back into her.

"Gray!" cries Dee.

"Too hard?"

"No, do it again."

When she doesn't protest, I pump in and out of her twice in quick succession. I continue my assault. This isn't lovemaking, this is claiming. I meant what I said, I love her, and from this day forward, she'll be mine forever.

Dee's pussy spasms around my cock, taking me by surprise. She likes it rough. Grunting, I spill my seed inside of her. "Dee!" I groan in pleasure.

When the last remnants of the orgasm subside, I pull out of her, and Dee whimpers.

"Did I hurt you?"

"Lord, no. That was unexpected but felt amazing."

Holding my hands out to her, we go into the bathroom. I turn on the shower and walk in under the icy spray. Dee waits until the water heats before she joins me. I soap up a washcloth and wash myself, and it's then I realize we didn't use protection.

"Shit."

Dee looks up at me. "What?"

"I didn't put on a condom."

"I'm on the pill."

Relief surges through me. "I'm glad one of us was thinking. That's the last thing either of us needs right now is a child. It would ruin everything."

"I know. I want to live with you for a few years and get to know you properly before we bring a child into the mix."

"Why didn't you tell me you were on the pill?"

"Safety first. It's always better to have two layers of protection, and besides, contraception shouldn't all be on me."

Pulling her to me, I kiss her. My girl is smart, and she knows a child right now isn't what's right for us. Unlike some of the other girls around campus, Dee isn't looking for a payday. Dee only wants me.

CHAPTER 7

DIANDRA

I'm late. It's Christmas Eve, and I'm supposed to be at Minerva's house for dinner. I've felt nauseous all day. Nothing seems to settle my stomach. The thought of eating a huge dinner causes my stomach to roll. I stop walking and lean up against a pillar near work to steady myself.

"Are you okay?"

Turning around, I find one of the agency's newest clients looking at me with concern.

"I think I have a stomach bug."

"You're Diandra, yes?" He takes me by my arm and guides me toward a bench.

"Yes. I'm sorry, I've forgotten your name, Mr.?"

"Tyson Reed, call me Tyson."

I nod, and my mouth waters, a sure sign I'm going to vomit.

"Oh my God," I mutter as I put my head between my knees.

"Please don't take this the wrong way, but you don't look good."

I'm sucking in mouthfuls of air to keep myself from losing my lunch all over Mr. Reed. He's some sort of self-made billionaire who wants another firm to look after his interests here in town.

"I'll be fine."

"Diandra, let me take you home."

Slowly, I straighten into a sitting position. "I'm supposed to be going out to dinner."

"Something tells me you aren't going to make it."

Groaning, I let my head fall back with my eyes closed. It's winter, and the cold air makes me feel slightly better. "I think you're right." Opening my eyes, I find Tyson peering over me. "I'm not dying, promise."

"You look green. Let me take you home. My driver is just over there." He points to a black limousine not twenty feet from us. "It's no trouble."

"My boyfriend and his mother are expecting me." I shake my head. "Who gets sick at Christmas?"

"Apparently, *you* do." Tyson stands and offers me his hand, which I gratefully take as I sluggishly get to my feet. Swiftly, he puts his arm around me and guides me toward his limousine.

"I'm sorry to be such a bother."

"Nonsense. I get to give a beautiful woman a ride home." He chuckles. "Even if she's a nice shade of green."

Smiling at him, I climb into his car and settle into the leather seats. Maybe it's because I'm not feeling well, but they are the softest seats I've ever sat in.

"Diandra, what's your address?"

"I'm over on Boylston Street, Boylston Apartments."

Closing my eyes, I feel the car move. Tyson doesn't make small talk, for which I'm grateful. The drive from work to home is less than fifteen minutes. The car stops, and my eyes fly open.

"You fell asleep."

"I'm so sorry. I never get sick."

"Don't be sorry," Tyson assures me as my door opens.

His driver is standing there, hand extended, waiting to help me out of the limousine. Nausea sweeps through me as I exit the car. I lean heavily against the back of it, breathing deeply.

"Give me your keys," orders Tyson.

Reaching into my bag, I dig through all of my belongings and eventually find my keys. Tyson takes them, then he puts an arm around me and helps me into my building. When we get inside my apartment, Tyson takes my bag, putting it on the small table near the door. I feel so tired—just putting one foot in front of the other is an effort. Stumbling, I walk into my bedroom.

"Let me help you take your coat off."

I do as I'm told and then flop onto the bed. Tyson kneels in front of me and slips off my shoes.

"Thank you. I've never felt like this before."

Tyson chuckles. "It's every man's dream to be told that in a woman's bedroom, but under these circumstances, it falls flat."

Next to my bed is a picture of Gray and me. Tyson picks it up as he stands.

"Your boyfriend is Grayson Moore?"

"Yes."

"Damn."

I frown at him. "Do you know Gray?"

"I'm the owner of the New England Warriors. We're in negotiations to sign him."

I smile weakly. "He's a good linebacker, you'll be lucky to have him."

"He certainly is a lucky bastard. He's got a long career ahead of him and a captivating girl to go home to."

"Gray doesn't live here."

Tyson pulls his cell phone out of his pocket, taps a number, and then puts it against his ear. I'm confused as to why he's still here. All I want to do is sleep.

"Grayson?" He pauses, listening to Gray. "Yes, it's Tyson Reed." Another pause. "I'm at your girlfriend, Diandra's place. I'm afraid she's not well. I think she has a stomach bug. She's a lovely shade of green." Tyson nods and then hands me the cell phone.

"Gray?"

"Babe, why didn't you call me?"

"I'm sorry. Mr. Reed drove me home from work. I don't think I'm going to make it tonight."

"Do you want me to come over?"

I shake my head. "No, I don't want you catching this. I'm sure I'll be fine tomorrow."

"I'll have dinner with Mom, then come over."

"You really don't have to."

"No, but I want to." I can hear the smile in his voice. "Mom says hello, and she'll see you tomorrow. I love you, Dee."

"I love you too."

Tyson takes the cell phone off me and puts it back to his ear. He smiles at me as he speaks to Gray.

"Her firm is handling some business for me. It was simply a happy coincidence." Tyson nods. "Good night, Gray."

"Thank you, Tyson, for seeing me home."

"Do you have a bucket?"

Frowning, I ask, "Why?"

Tyson looks around my bedroom. "You don't look well and might not make it to the bathroom."

"Oh." Tyson smiles, and I shake my head. "No, I don't."

"Do you mind if I have a look in your kitchen?"

I shake my head, and he walks out of my bedroom. Laying back on the bed, I pull a blanket over myself and close my eyes. I'm so tired, and my stomach, for now, seems to have settled.

My last thought is how nice Tyson Reed is to help a virtual stranger and that it's unusual, especially considering he's not known for being nice. He's a ruthless business executive. He even talked my boss into giving him a discount.

The next morning, I wake up with Gray snoring lightly beside me. Rolling over, I put my feet on the floor, and next to the bed is a large bowl. I'm guessing Tyson put that there. Standing, a wave of nausea sweeps through me, and I run for the bathroom. With my head over the toilet bowl, I bring up what little is in my stomach.

"Oh, honey," coos Gray as he holds my hair back.

"S-Sorry," I blurt out as my body tries to expel everything out of me.

"No need to apologize."

Gray leaves me for a moment and comes back with a washcloth, which he runs under the cold water tap and hands it to me. I wipe my face and sit down next to the toilet.

"I didn't even hear you come in last night."

"Tyson Reed let me in. You were out."

"He stayed?"

Gray nods. "Yeah, he seems like a good guy."

"How was dinner with your mom?"

"She's worried about you."

"Honestly, it's just a bug."

"Can I get you something to eat?"

My stomach turns over on itself at the thought of food. "Ugh, no."

"I'm going to ring my mom."

I fold the washcloth in half and put it across my eyes. Gray's footsteps tell me he's back in the room, and then I feel him sit next to me.

"I'm going to get you water, and Mom said dry toast will help settle you."

"I need a shower."

"You're still in your work clothes."

I pull the cloth off my face and look down. "Yep."

Gray stands and holds out his hands to me. "Come on, let's get you naked and clean."

"I'm so sorry, Gray." He pulls me to my feet. "It's not the best way to spend Christmas."

"I forgot." His face lights up. "Merry Christmas, beautiful." Gray kisses me on the forehead. "Do you need help in the shower?"

"No. I'll be fine."

He kisses me again and leaves me alone. Looking at my reflection in the mirror, my hair is standing up in all different directions, and I have circles under my eyes.

"Damn, you look bad," I whisper to myself.

Gray pops his head back into the bathroom. "Did you say something?"

"Just talking to myself." I lock eyes with him in the mirror. "You should be with your mom."

"I will be, a little later. I need to make sure you're okay first. It's our second Christmas together. We need to make it special."

"Me throwing up is super special."

Gray laughs. "It's definitely different."

After my shower, I feel a little better. Wrapping myself up in my fluffy, pink bathrobe, I walk into my kitchen to find Gray has made coffee and toast and strung up some tinsel.

"Aww, thank you, baby."

He also has tinsel draped around his neck.

"Do you feel better?"

"Yeah."

Gray hands me a coffee, and I hold it up to my nose and inhale its rich scent. My stomach doesn't protest, so I take a small sip.

"Go sit on the couch, and I'll bring everything in."

Sitting down, I tuck my feet up underneath me and wait for Gray. He comes in with a plate of toast and a coffee cup in his hand.

"Do you want your present now?"

Instantly forgetting my nausea, I say, "Now!"

Gray laughs, hands me the toast, and puts his coffee cup down. I have a small tree set up in the corner of my apartment. Gray goes over to the tree and pulls out a tiny, navy box from its branches.

"How long has that been hidden in there?"

Gray shrugs. "A while. It was safer to hide it here than at home or with my mom."

"Yours is the big red box."

Gray retrieves his present and puts it on my coffee table. "You first."

The little velvet box has a silver ribbon tied around it. I undo the ribbon and open the box. Inside is a gold band with engraving around it. I take the ring out of the box, and on the inside of it are the words, *Promise, love Gray.*

Gray takes the ring from me and puts it on my right ring finger. "It's a promise ring. But it's more than that. It's my vow to you. I love you, Dee, and when I've established myself, and I'm worthy of you, you'll be mine forever."

Tears well in my eyes as I stare at the intricate gold band on my finger. "It's beautiful, Gray." A tear escapes and falls down my cheek. "But you *are* worthy." I throw my arms around him. "I love it, thank you."

"Everything is falling into place, Dee. Everything I've worked for is coming together. We're going to have the best life."

"Gray, we have a good life."

"It will be better. Once I've established myself and you've got your dream job."

It all comes back to his five-year plan. He says he'd change it all in a heartbeat for me, but I know he's worked too hard for too long to do that. And I'd never ask him to. Looking down at the ring, I know it's his way of telling me he loves me and that, in time, we'll get married. Maybe it's the fact I'm not feeling well or that it's Christmas, the first one I haven't spent with my family, but I wish Gray didn't find it necessary to plan everything in his life down to the last detail.

"Open yours."

Gray rips the wrapping off the box, then removes the lid. Inside is a charcoal-colored cashmere sweater that cost me a small fortune. Gray pulls it out, letting the box fall to the floor.

Gray holds the soft sweater to his face for a moment, then cups my face in his hands. "I love it."

"Really?"

"Yeah, babe, it's perfect."

Getting up off the couch, I retrieve his Christmas card from under the tree.

With a smilie, I hand it over to Gray. He takes it off me and weighs it in his hand.

"There's something else inside of here."

"Just a little something extra."

Gray rips open the envelope, and a small silver necklace with a pendant falls out of the card. It's Scrosoppi, the patron saint of footballers, and on the back I had them engrave a G, a heart, and a D.

He holds it up, a smile creeps across his face. "The sweater was nice, but this, this is amazing. I love it."

"To keep you safe on the field."

"With you, my mom, football, and this, what could go wrong?"

CHAPTER 8

DIANDRA

Four days later, I'm sitting in my doctor's office. I've felt ill for days. The gods smiled down on me, and I was lucky to get an appointment between Christmas and New Year's—the kind receptionist squeezed me in. Dr. Hale is an older lady. I've seen her a few times since I've lived here. She's always very blunt and to the point. My stomach won't settle. It doesn't seem to matter what I eat or drink or think about, I feel horrible, so she's taken some blood and a urine sample.

The door opens, and Dr. Hale walks in. She gives me a tight smile as she takes her place behind her desk. "How are you feeling?"

"The same as before. Queasy. Do I have a bug, Doc?"

Dr. Hale arranges her hands on her desk and smiles at me. "When was your last menstrual cycle?"

No.

Shit, I'm late.

Dr. Hale nods at me. "Yes, Diandra, you're pregnant."

"I'm on the pill."

Dr. Hale nods again. "It's not infallible. It has the potential to be ninety-nine percent effective. Nine out of one hundred women fall pregnant while on the pill every year."

"No," I whisper.

Dr. Hale pushes some pamphlets toward me on the desk. "You're young. There are options. You can choose to keep the child, you could put it up for adoption, or you can terminate the pregnancy. You have time to decide."

Glancing down, I look at Gray's promise ring. This isn't in *his* plan.

"Diandra?" I look up at Dr. Hale. "Do you have family? Is the young man still in the picture?"

"He doesn't want children yet. He's got a five-year plan, and this isn't part of his plan."

Dr. Hale smiles. "Well, not everything goes to plan. Sometimes we have to make changes."

"You don't understand." I pick up the pamphlets off her desk. "He's worked his entire life to get where he is. This would ruin everything."

"Talk to the young man. You don't have to go through this on your own. Do you have family close by?"

"My mom lives here, and my dad lives in New York."

"Good. It's good you have a support system."

I stand, slightly dazed and not knowing what to do.

"Diandra?"

"Hmm?"

"The morning sickness should stop at about fourteen weeks. Until then, dry toast and crackers. There's been some research to suggest ginger will help alleviate the symptoms." Dr. Hale stands and walks around her desk. "I know before my pregnancy, I used to love tuna, but while pregnant, I couldn't stand the smell. We're all different. If you keep the baby, you might have cravings, but remember, everything in moderation."

"Thanks, Dr. Hale." I hold up the pamphlets and walk out of her office.

I keep walking, not knowing where I'm going. Eventually, I find myself on my mother's doorstep. I knock on the red wooden door, and Mom opens it. Her face turns into one big smile, and she hugs me.

"Well, this is unexpected! What are you doing here, baby girl?"

Mom guides me to her kitchen table, and I sit down. The pamphlets from the doctor's office are still in my hands, and I put them in front of her.

Mom frowns, then picks one up, then another, and another. Her eyes well with tears, then she drops them and grasps my hands. "Say it's not so."

I nod, unable to speak.

"Oh, honey, what are you going to do? Have you told Grayson?"

"No, and promise me you won't tell anyone," I plead.

"It's Grayson's problem too."

"You don't understand, Mom. He's wanted to play professional ball his entire life, this will complicate things."

Tears course down her face. "Honey, you can't do this on your own. Grayson loves you."

"He does, and I love him. But I need to decide what's best for *me*. Promise me, Mom, you won't tell a soul."

Mom puts both hands to her face and wipes away her tears. "You've always known what to do." She reaches out and puts one of her hands over mine. "You've never been a bother even when Daddy and I got divorced. I sometimes felt like you were the grownup." She sighs. "If you want to keep it a secret, no matter what you decide, I'm here for you, honey."

The tears I'd been holding in spill over, and sobs wrack my body.

Mom instantly stands and holds me to her, both of us crying and clinging to each other. When I'm done, Mom drags her chair closer to me and sits down. She picks up one of the pamphlets on abortion, and her lips turn down. "Do you know what you want to do?"

I shake my head. "No." I take the brochure off her and toss it further away on the table. "But not that. I don't think I can do that."

Mom pats my arm. "Whatever you decide, I'm here for you."

"And you can't tell Minerva."

Mom's mouth drops open slightly, then she clamps it shut and nods. "I won't even tell your daddy if you don't want me to."

"Thanks, Mom. I love you."

"Oh, sugar, I love you to the moon and back."

I'm standing downwind of Bruno's food truck. The smell of hotdogs makes me ill. Dr. Hale was right, ginger tea settles my stomach. I made some and have it in a to-go cup while I wait for Gray.

It's been two days since my appointment with the doctor. There never seems to be a good time to tell Gray. He's received an offer from the New England Warriors, and it's all he can talk about.

I see Gray in the distance. He's with Colton, and the pair of them are laughing. When he sees me, Gray jogs toward me with Colton following close behind.

"Hey, baby." He kisses my lips, takes my to-go cup out of my hand, takes a sip, then spits it out. "*What* is that?"

"Ginger tea."

Colt and I both laugh at him. "That's it, laugh it up, you two. I'm going to grab a hotdog, do you want one?"

"No." My stomach still isn't great.

"Colt?"

"You buying?" Gray nods at him. "Then, yes, I'll have one with the lot."

Colt puts his arm around me and guides me to a seat.

"Keep your hands off my girl, you're in enough trouble as it is!" yells Gray.

I giggle as we sit. Colt makes a big show of sitting close to me.

"He's so jealous."

"Can you blame him? You're not exactly the shy, quiet type."

Colt feigns shock with his mouth hanging open and a hand dramatically clutching his chest. "You wound me!"

"Colton Anders, you should've studied acting."

Colt drops the façade and nods. "Maybe?"

I chuckle at him. "Why are you in trouble?"

"Ahh, you caught that, did you?" Colt moves slightly away from me and picks up a leaf from the table, twirling it in his fingers. "Do you remember Cindy?"

"Downward dog, Cindy?"

Colt rolls his eyes. "Yeah, that's her." He tosses the leaf away and clasps his hands together on the table. "She had a pregnancy scare."

"Is she?"

"No, no!" Colt shakes his head vigorously. "I'm out of the woods." He nods toward Gray. "It was touch and go for a couple of days, but Gray helped me through it. We came up with a game plan if she was pregnant."

Glancing at Gray, I ask, "What was the game plan?"

"Gray said a baby would ruin everything for me, and he's right. Can you imagine having a baby now? We've both been signed with the New England Warriors, and it's not the time to be having kids, especially with a girl like Cindy."

I bristle at his comment and scowl at him. "A girl like Cindy?"

Colt nods. "Yeah, who'd want to have a kid now? We're just getting started. The next few years are all about establishing ourselves, striving forward. Like Gray said, no one wants to be tied to some girl he has a fling with in college for the rest of his life because of a kid. Anyway, it doesn't matter. False alarm." Colt lets out a long breath. "I'm free."

"Gray said that a baby would ruin everything?"

Gray flops onto the bench seat opposite us, handing Colt his hotdog. "It sure would. Our boy here got lucky!" Gray grins. "Can you imagine having a kid now?" He shakes his head. "Professional suicide, no one wants to do a sponsorship deal with a guy who can't handle his business. I made him go to a lawyer and draw up papers to protect himself." Whatever Gray sees on my face, he reaches over and takes my hand. "Cindy is a nice girl, but how do we know it was his? Colt needed to make sure he had all his bases covered."

"So it would've been Cindy's problem?"

Gray nods at me. "Until the paperwork came back saying it was his, but all this is moot, she's not pregnant, and Colt, here, is going to be more careful from now on. Isn't that right?"

"Damn straight," agrees Colt. "We're way too young to be having children. Your mom would kill me."

Gray chuckles. "You got that right. She'd whoop both our asses. You for not being careful and me for not watching out for you."

"Because a child would ruin everything?"

Gray and Colt both nod as they devour their hotdogs. My heart sinks. There's no way I can tell him I'm pregnant. He'll either think I am after a payday or that I'm trying to ruin his life. Sipping my tea, I watch them both eat. It seems like the two of them have it all figured out. If the girl gets pregnant, you draw up papers protecting yourself, treating her like she's the enemy.

"Dee? Dee, are you listening?" Gray is waving a hand in my face.

Shaking myself, I shake my head. "What?"

"You're coming tonight, aren't you?"

Tyson Reed is hosting a big celebration party to welcome the new blood into the team. Gray and Colt are the guests of honor.

"I wouldn't miss it for the world."

CHAPTER 9

DIANDRA

Tyson Reed's New Year's Eve party is at one of the hottest nightclubs in town. I'm wearing a red, glittery dress with a V-neck, and I've paired it with six-inch black heels. Gray's mouth actually dropped open when he came to pick me up.

"Red looks good on you," compliments Tyson Reed.

Blushing, I smile at him. "Thank you. And thanks for inviting us to the party." Reaching out, I touch his arm. "And thank you for looking after me on Christmas Eve. It's so nice of you."

"I've always wanted to be the knight in shining armor." He chuckles. "And this party is for the team. The new get to meet the old players. An ice-breaker before I start to change things up. Are you having a good time?"

He offers me a glass of champagne, but I shake my head. "No."

"Stomach still upset?"

"You could say that."

Tyson raises an eyebrow. "Is everything okay, Diandra?"

"Tonight is for the boys... it's not about me."

Tyson drinks one of the glasses of champagne and puts the glass on a passing server's tray.

"This sounds serious. Care to share?"

Tyson is good-looking, and he knows it, so I smile and shake my head. My emotions are far too close to the surface to have this conversation with him, especially as I haven't told Gray, and I'm not sure I ever will. Tyson grabs me by the upper arm and leads me to the VIP section. No one else is in here, and he guides me to a small table. The noise level in here is much quieter. A server comes up, and Tyson orders a whiskey neat even though he still has a glass of champagne on the table.

"Diandra, have you eaten?"

"I'm fine."

"That's not what I asked."

"My stomach still hasn't settled."

Tyson looks at the server. "Find me some saltines or dry crackers for the lady, please."

"Yes, sir."

I wait until the server is gone before I hiss at him, "You didn't need to do that."

"No, I didn't, but your face is a little pale, and I want you to have a good time."

Crossing my legs, I get more comfortable in the chair. "This must have cost a fortune."

"I've signed some of the hottest rising stars in the league. They should get spoiled before the fun starts."

"The fun?"

"Oh, I expect them to bring me the Super Bowl Championship trophy. Not this year, but within the next three years." He sips his champagne. "I expect them to train hard."

"It's all Gray wants too," I reply sadly.

Tyson frowns. "It's a good thing, is it not? He impressed me with his goals. So far, he has achieved everything he's set out to do."

"Yeah."

Tyson reaches across the table and touches my hand briefly. "What's wrong?"

I uncross my legs, sit a little straighter in the chair, and shake my head. "Nothing."

"Tsk, tsk." Tyson stares into my eyes. "I promise not to tell anyone. Your secrets are safe with me."

I open and close my mouth twice, then blurt out, "I'm pregnant."

As those words seem to hang in the air, I wrap my arms around myself. My throat burns as I hold back tears, not knowing how I'm going to tell Gray or his mother or if I ever will. Tyson stands and once again, grabs me by my upper arm, leading me further into the VIP section. We come to a door, and he opens it, taking us out onto a balcony and into the frosty night air. Immediately, he takes off his coat and drapes it around me.

"How far along are you? What are you going to do?"

"I'm eleven weeks, and I don't know. Gray has all these plans, and this will ruin everything he's worked for." Tears fall down my face as I stare out over the lights of the city.

"Wait here," orders Tyson as he goes back into the club.

He comes back a few moments later with napkins and hands them to me. "We don't want to ruin your makeup."

Tyson is quiet for a while, letting me cry without bombarding me with questions.

"I'm so sorry, I shouldn't have told you that," I whisper.

"Don't be sorry, I asked." Tyson looks down at me, then away at the city. "You could get rid of it."

It's not something I haven't thought of, but the very idea is appalling to me. "No, I can't."

"Gray doesn't know?"

I shake my head.

"When I was in your boss's office, he shared he wanted you to move to New York to work in their office. Is this something you've considered?"

"Yes and no. Gray was hoping you'd sign him, and if you did, I was going to get a job here to be close to him, but a baby will ruin everything for him. Gray will want to do the right thing, and he'll want to marry me." I look up into Tyson's eyes. "I want to marry him, but not like this. Gray has it all planned out, and this isn't part of his plan."

"Plans can change."

I look back out over the city and shake my head. "No, it's not fair to Gray."

"What about you?"

Looking down at my feet, I shrug. "I don't know."

Tyson is quiet, then he paces back and forth in front of me. "I have an idea." He stops pacing and grips me by the shoulders. "I could help. You could take the job in New York. Gray will never know you were pregnant. You could have the baby there, and when the time is right for *you and Gray*, then you can tell him everything."

"How would you help?"

"I have an apartment in New York. You could live there for free. Gray need never know about the baby."

"Why would you help a complete stranger?"

Tyson rubs my arms, then lets his arms fall to his sides. "I'm able to do it, and I'm looking after my investment in Gray. If you think about it, I'm being a selfish bastard."

"You won't tell him?"

"Not unless you want me to."

Taking a deep breath, I slowly let it out and nod at Tyson. "I'll pay you back."

Tyson smiles and shakes his head. "Not necessary."

"How much money do you have?"

Tyson shrugs, a smile spreads across his face. "Enough to waste it on a football team."

I laugh. "That much, huh?"

"When do you want to do this?"

The reality of the situation comes crashing down on me, and I shiver at the thought of leaving Gray. "I'm not sure I can leave him."

"It will only be temporary, just until you both are settled into your careers. I've seen the way Gray looks at you, everything will work out for the best in the end."

It all seems so simple.

But how do I leave the man I love?

How do I do all of this on my own?

"This is crazy. And I don't need your help, Tyson. My dad lives in New York. I could stay with him."

"How big is your dad's place?"

Sighing, I frown. "It's two bedrooms, one bathroom."

Tyson nods. "I have a five-bedroom apartment that I never use. It overlooks Central Park, perfect for taking a baby on strolls. I think I've been there twice this year. And if I wanted to stay, I could be in the other wing, and you'd never even know I was there."

"Wing?"

Tyson smiles. "It's big."

He's gazing at me, and I'm confused as to why this complete stranger would help me.

"You know it's getting cold out here, and Gray is going to wonder where you are. You don't have to decide now. We can talk about it some more."

Swaying from side to side, I nod once and then say, "No strings. This is strictly a business arrangement. I *will* pay you back. And I'd appreciate it if you said nothing to Gray or his mother."

"It's none of my business." Tyson turns me around and opens the door. "Maybe you could do some accounting for me as payment?"

"I can do that."

Tyson smiles. "Sounds like you've made up your mind. When do you want to leave?"

"Soon. I'm already starting to show."

Tyson looks me up and down and shakes his head. "No, you're not. I can arrange for someone to come to your apartment and pack it up for you. All you need to do is pack a bag when you're ready to leave, and I'll take care of the rest."

Tears well in my eyes, and he shuts the door.

"No more tears. It's one of the happiest nights of Grayson's life. Let's not spoil it for him."

I nod, suck in a deep breath, and open the door.

As we make our way back into the club, I spot Gray instantly and give him a little wave. He comes bounding over and then frowns at me.

"Nice coat?"

I shrug it off and hand it to Tyson. "I wasn't feeling well, and Tyson took me out to the balcony for some fresh air, but it was cold out there."

Gray puts his hands on my shoulder and dips his head to stare into my eyes. "Are you okay?"

I nod.

"She's fine. I think that stomach bug is still hanging around."

"Thanks, Mr. Reed, for looking after her."

I find it odd that I call him Tyson, but Gray calls him Mr. Reed.

"It's no problem, Grayson. You've got a good woman there." He pats me on the shoulder as he goes back into the throng of people.

"I think he likes you," teases Gray.

"He knows I'm your girl."

"He better."

CHAPTER 10

DIANDRA

Six Months Later

My lower back is killing me. My little man is kicking up a storm today. I'm in my office, it's the smallest office in Mr. Brookes' agency, more like a cupboard, but it has a window. Not that I have a great view unless you call looking at the adjacent building a view. My boss, Mr. Brookes, wasn't happy when he found out I was pregnant, but Tyson fixed things for me. He's been a godsend. Not only has he let me live in his apartment, but he keeps me up to date on Gray. Tyson visits at least once a week with gifts for my little man and sometimes me. I'm not stupid, I know Tyson likes me. Many times, I've explained to him that I love Gray, and he nods, but know he's hoping I'll one day look at him and change my mind.

That's never going to happen.

There's a knock at my door and one of the interns, Sally, pokes her head in. "How you doing?"

"My back is killing me," I groan.

"Want a heat pack?"

"Oh, yes, please."

Sally winks at me and disappears. Leaning forward, I rub my lower back as best I can. One of the worst things about pregnancy, apart from the nausea that never went away, is the back pain. Well, that and the fact everyone assumes they can touch my ever-growing belly. Complete strangers come up and touch it—it's like it has become public property. I don't like it.

Sally opens my door and comes in with a wheat pack. I stand, and as I do, I feel a pop, and then water gushes down my legs. "Oh, my God!" I gasp.

"What?" exclaims Sally.

"I think my water just broke!"

Sally drops the wheat bag onto my desk. "What do you want me to do?"

"I don't know!"

Sally takes my hands. "Okay, we've got this. Who do we call?"

"Tyson." I pick up my cell phone and call him.

"Diandra?"

"My water broke."

"Where are you?"

"At work."

"Go to the hospital. I'll be there as soon as I can."

He hangs up, and I look at Sally. "He said to go to the hospital."

"Sounds like a good plan. I'll come with you."

I nod and pick up my handbag, which Sally takes off me.

"Do you have a go-bag?"

"It's at home." Tears well in my eyes.

"Don't do that, Diandra. Everything is going to be fine. Deep breaths. Let's get you to the hospital."

I nod and let her guide me out of the office, into the elevator, and out onto the sidewalk. Sally hails a cab and puts me in it, then runs to the other side to get in.

"Is she having a baby?" asks the cabbie aggressively.

"Yes, she is. So step on it!"

The cabbie harrumphs and pulls out into traffic. "Which hospital? If she makes a mess back there, I'm charging you for the cleaning."

"That's fine. Montlake Hospital on thirtieth and thirty-third streets." Pain far worse than any cramps I've ever had rip through me, and I gasp. "Jesus Christ!"

"Remember to breathe," says Sally.

I've done all the classes, but nothing prepared me for this. I'm panting, making all the stupid noises, and Sally is rubbing my lower back. The contraction eases, and I look at the cabbie in his rearview mirror.

"I'll give you my card. If you need to have the car cleaned, please bill me."

"Damn straight, I will."

"Thank you for being so *nice*," replies Sally with attitude.

The cabbie pulls into the emergency room entrance, and Sally gets out and runs around the car to help me. She tosses money at the cabbie along with my business card. "You have a nice day," she mutters as she helps me into the hospital.

It's a private hospital, so there aren't many people in the emergency room.

Sally leaves me to run up to a nurse. "She's having a baby!" Sally points at me as I walk toward the receptionist counter.

The older nurse smiles at Sally. "Calm down. Women have babies every day." She comes over, and I smile at her. "How you doing, honey?"

"My water broke, and I think I just had my first contraction."

"You think?" she laughs. "I'm Judy. I am a nurse here. Are you booked in?"

"My doctor is Tremaine Lock. I don't have my bag and..." bursting into tears, I say, "... I'm all alone."

Judy's face softens. "You're not alone, honey. I'm here, your girlfriend is here. Everything is going to be all right." Judy looks at Sally. "Can you get her bag?"

Sally looks at me. "Do you want me to?"

I nod. "Yes, please. Take my handbag, I've got money in my purse, and my house keys are in there too."

"I don't know where you live."

"The Beresford, Central Park West, the doorman's name is Fred. Apartment nine D, E."

"Fancy," says Judy.

I nod repeatedly. "It's not mine. When you get out of the elevator, take the first door on your right and go to the end of the hallway... that's my room. The bag is on a chair near the window. It's black."

The apartment is huge. It's five bedrooms, six bathrooms, and more living areas than I could or would ever need. Tyson offered to redecorate it for me, but I only use half of the apartment. Not even all of the half. It's seventy-five five hundred square feet of luxury—far too much space for one person. Tyson said he got it for a steal, but it would've cost millions.

"Okay! I'm on it." Sally is fluttering her hands all over the place and not moving.

Smiling at her, I reach out and touch her arm. "Tell Fred I'm fine."

"Fred?"

"My doorman. Ask him to go with you. He's helped me more than once with groceries."

"Are you sure you're going to be okay?"

"Sally, I'm in the best place to have a baby. Trust me, Tyson looked into everything."

Sally lets out a breath, kisses my cheek, and runs for the door.

"She's a nervous little thing, ain't she?" asks Judy.

"She's young, and it's her first baby."

"You two aren't a couple, though, are you?"

Laughing, I shake my head. "No. She's an intern where I work."

"Is Tyson your baby daddy?"

"No, ma'am, he's a friend. He is on his way."

Judy smiles at me. I smile back, but then another contraction hits, and I'm sure my smile looks more like a grimace as I groan in pain.

"Come on, honey, let's get you into a chair and to your room."

An hour later, I'm in my private room as another contraction tears through my body. I'm tired. I've had enough, and my little man isn't here yet.

A worried Tyson comes flying into the room. He immediately puts an arm around me and starts to breathe deeply. "In and out, like we practiced."

"I don't think I can do this."

Tyson chuckles. "Too late now, Diandra."

The contraction fades, and I relax back into the bed. "It hurts."

"No one said it was going to be easy."

Scowling at him, I close my eyes.

"Do you want me to call Gray?"

Opening my eyes, tears form, and I shake my head. "No. You said he's only just settling down. He needs to find his feet with the New England Warriors before I tell him he's got a son."

At first, Tyson was all for not telling Gray about my pregnancy, but as the months wore on and he could see how unhappy I am, he changed his mind. Tyson doesn't like to see me upset or sad, which is sweet. He's going to make a wonderful godfather.

"If you change your mind, let me know."

Judy comes into the room with my black bag and handbag. "Sally left this at the desk for you. She said to say she had to go back to work."

"Why didn't you tell me you didn't have your bag? I could've gotten it for you."

"You weren't here, and Sally was."

Judy puts my bags down and walks over to me. "How are you feeling, honey?"

"The pain is horrible."

Judy smiles and nods. "Has your doctor been to see you yet?"

I shake my head.

"Dr. Lock hasn't been to see you?" asks Tyson as he pulls his cell phone out of his pocket.

"Not yet. I've only been here for an hour."

"And I'm not paying him a small fortune *not* to be here."

Reaching out to Tyson, I put my hand on his arm. "I'm okay."

"You just said you were in horrible pain. That's *not* okay."

Judy pats my arm. "If you need anything, you buzz the nurses' station. I'm finished for the day. Good luck."

Judy leaves the room, and Tyson has his phone against his ear, talking quietly to whoever is on the other end. My gasp of pain causes him to drop his cell phone and grab my hand.

"What can I do?" His face is a mask of concern.

Tyson was also my Lamaze partner, so when I begin to pant, he does the same. His hand goes to my lower back, and he rubs up and down soothingly. Slowly, the contraction fades, and I lock eyes with him.

"What did Dr. Lock say?"

Tyson looks down at the floor where his cell phone is lying. "He said he'd be here shortly."

"Good."

"I'm here for you. If you need anything, you need only ask."

"Tyson, you've done so much for me already. I don't know how I'd have made it these past few months without you."

Tyson smiles. "You have no idea how much I've enjoyed being a part of this. And like I told you in the beginning, I'm a selfish bastard who simply wanted to keep his star linebacker from losing concentration, or worse yet, backing out of the contract."

"Keep telling yourself that, but I know better."

"Pfft," replies Tyson.

I don't respond to his flippant reply as another contraction hits me.

My labor lasted seven hours. Dawson Tyson Evergrow entered this world at three seventeen in the morning, weighing eight pounds twelve ounces, and he looks just like his daddy.

Tyson was with me through all of it. He even cut the cord. Tyson is a good man and will be a wonderful role model for my son. Right now, he's standing beside my bed, rocking Dawson. He is swaying from side to side, cooing at my small bundle of life. Seeing him with Dawson, I finally understand that Gray can never know he has a son. He'll never forgive me for not sharing this with him. A single tear runs down my cheek, and Tyson stops moving.

"Are you in pain? Do you want me to get the doctor?"

"No, I'm fine. I just wish Gray was here."

Tyson nods but says nothing. For the past seven hours, we've had the same conversation many times. Hell, since I moved to New York, we've had this conversation repeatedly. Tyson thinks Gray should know. Maybe when Dawson is older and wants to get to know his father, I'll tell Gray. Until then, it's just us.

CHAPTER 11

DIANDRA

Present Day

The flight back to New York seemed to take forever, then battling traffic to get to the hospital felt like an eternity. Now, as I walk back into the hospital where I gave birth to my son all those years ago, sadness fills me.

I deserved every horrible thing that Gray said to me. Every harsh look, but I was hoping he'd see me and remember what we once had.

That he once loved me.

That, at one time, he wanted to build a life with me.

If I'd known then what I know now, I would have told him. Dawson needs him, and for my son, I would sacrifice anything, and I have, with Tyson's help. Once Dawson was born, he helped me get the financing to open my own agency. Without him guaranteeing everything, the banks wouldn't have touched me. To this day, I still look after his interests in New York for free. Although Tyson never invested in me financially, I wouldn't be where I am without him. Tyson gave me a place to stay, opened doors, and supported me emotionally. He's good friend.

The hospital feels too quiet as I make my way to Dawson's room. My mom and dad stayed with him while I was away. The door to his room is open. Peeking in, I find my mom and dad asleep in chairs, but Dawson is sitting up staring at a teddy bear. His eyes light up when he sees me. "Mommy!"

I hold my finger to my lips and pad softly into the room. Neither Mom or Dad wake up as I sit on his bed.

"What have you got there, big man?" I whisper.

"Tyson gave it to me."

I cock my head to the side. "When did he give you that?"

"Just before."

"Is he here?"

"He said he's going to get a hot chocolate, but I think he's getting coffee." Dawson's little lips turn down. He doesn't like coffee.

I laugh. "Why would he say hot chocolate if he's getting coffee?"

"To trick me!" Dawson giggles.

"Shh." I glance at my parents, but they are still sleeping. "Did you miss me?"

Dawson nods his head vigorously. "Did you see my dad?"

"Yeah, baby, and he's coming to visit."

"He is?"

"Yes, *and* he's bringing his mom, so you'll have another granny."

"Do I get another grandpa too?"

"No, you won't. You're super lucky and just get me," teases my dad as he stands and hugs me.

"Hey, Dad."

"When did you get back?"

"Just now." I smile down at Dawson. "Did he have a rough night?"

Dad rubs the top of Dawson's head. "Yeah, big man here couldn't sleep. Your mom and I stayed up with him. I guess we both dropped off."

Mom groans as she straightens up in her chair. "He missed his momma."

"Grams, you snored."

My mother straightens her shoulders and pushes her hair out of her face. "I do *not* snore."

Dawson giggles. "Yes, you did!"

"Now, Dawson, your grams does not snore, she simply breathes loudly." Dad smiles at Mom, and she blushes.

He has always had a way with the ladies. It's one of the reasons they got divorced. Dad couldn't keep his hands to himself, and one day Mom simply had enough of his philandering ways.

"How did it go, honey? What did Grayson have to say?"

"Did you see they won, Mom?" interjects Dawson.

I position myself next to him on the bed and tuck him into my side. "Yes, honey, I saw." I stare at Mom. "He's coming, so is Minerva."

Mom's face clouds over. "She's going to be so cross with me."

I shake my head. "No, Mom. I explained it to her. She's hurt, but she can't wait to meet Dawson." I tickle under his arm, and he laughs.

Dawson looks up at me and yawns. As part of his disease he gets tired easily, so I'm a little surprised he didn't sleep with me being gone.

"How about you close your eyes, little man?"

"You'll be here when I wake up?"

"I'm never leaving you again." I kiss the top of his head, and he yawns.

"Okay, Momma." Dawson closes his eyes, and within moments, his little mouth falls open, and he's asleep.

"How bad was it?" asks my mom.

I let out a breath and move off Dawson's bed. "He's mad. Minerva is excited." I give Mom a forced smile.

"Did you explain to him why you left?"

I shake my head. "No. He didn't give me a chance."

"Well, you hurt him pretty badly, Diandra," says Tyson as he comes into the room with what I assume are four cups of coffee.

"Did you get a hot chocolate?" I ask with a grin.

"He ratted me out?" Tyson laughs.

"Gray will be here soon." I take a coffee off Tyson. "I don't think you should be here. He was furious."

Tyson purses his lips and then looks at Dawson. "Yeah, he has a right to be. Did he say he'd do it?"

The moment we were told that Dawson needed a kidney transplant, Tyson got tested. He's not a match.

"He wants a paternity test first."

Tyson's mouth drops open, and my mother gasps.

Holding up my hands, I turn so I'm facing everyone. "He has a right. Gray didn't know I was pregnant, let alone had a child. The main thing is... he's coming. We'll deal with everything else as it comes. Dawson is our only priority."

Tyson hands out the other coffees to my parents. His jaw is ticking, which means he's angry. My dad is also looking at me with his lips turned down.

"At the end of the day, this is all on me. I should've told Gray. I know you all think that too." Looking down at my feet, I take a deep breath and look at the people I love most in the world. "I thought I was doing what was best for Gray, but it has backfired horribly. If I could take it all back, I would."

Mom embraces me. "Oh, honey, Gray is a good man. Well, he was. I'm sure he'll do the right thing."

Five hours later, and I'm waiting nervously for Gray and his mom in the hospital lobby. I told my parents and Tyson to leave, as I don't want any tension when they arrive. Unfortunately, that means I have to deal with Gray by myself. My stomach is in knots as I wait for them. Dawson was asleep when I slipped out of his room. His color doesn't look as good today, and I think he's lost a little more weight.

Gray is the first one through the doors. He's wearing jeans, a dark jacket, and a white shirt. Minerva has on a pale blue pantsuit. Both look frazzled, or maybe it's annoyance? Gray isn't the man I knew anymore. He was never cold or said things to deliberately hurt me, but I suppose I only have myself to blame.

Minerva is the first to see me. With determination, she strides toward me, wrapping her arms around my frame, holding me tightly. It's a comfort, I didn't know I needed.

"How is he?"

"He's holding his own. Dawson was asleep when I left."

Gray stands behind his mother. He's gotten broader and filled out more since we were in college together. He lets out a sigh and runs a hand through his short, cropped hair.

"Okay, we're here," he says in a flat monotone.

Minerva turns around quickly and gives him a stern look, her mouth a hard, thin line. "*Grayson.*"

He looks at his mother and shrugs, a silent war going on between them.

Gray won't even look at me.

I clear my throat, and Minerva grabs my hand.

"Would you like to meet him?" I ask her.

"Oh, yes. Very much." Minerva links arms with me, and I walk her through the hospital. Many of the staff say hello to me as I pass.

"You're here a lot?" asks Gray.

"Yes. Dawson is here full-time now."

"That must be expensive."

"Grayson Moore! You mind your tongue," hisses Minerva.

"It's okay." I pat her arm. "It's expensive, but we get by."

Gray grunts and follows us from behind. His anger is like an armor he's wearing to protect himself. My only hope is he's nice to Dawson.

CHAPTER 12

GRAYSON

I saw her the minute we entered the hospital. Motherhood has done nothing to diminish her beauty. Diandra is still the center of the universe, and the rest of us gravitate toward her. More than one person stopped to look at her. Diandra has always had a presence.

Not wanting to appear too interested, I pretended not to see her, but my mother almost ran to Diandra the moment her eyes landed on her. Dee barely looked at me. She's not wearing a ring, but a woman like her probably didn't stay single for long. The thought of her with another man makes me angry. When I join them, I run a hand through my hair to ease some of the tension within my body.

As we walk to her son's room, many hospital staff greet her by name and say hello. This means she must spend a lot of time here. This is a private hospital, so the medical bills alone must be crippling her. It makes me wonder how she can afford it. I did some digging on the plane, and she does have a lucrative accounting firm, but even so, all of her money must be tied up in keeping her son alive.

Diandra comes to a stop at what I presume is Dawson's room. She positions herself in front of me, a frown on her beautiful face.

"Dawson is only three. He knows you're his daddy, and he's a huge fan." She closes the gap between us and rests her hands on my chest. "Please be nice to him, Gray, he has been through so much. He's innocent in all of this."

Her hands on my chest make my heart beat faster, and a warmth spreads through me. This woman destroyed me once, and it seems she still has power over me. I close my eyes and shake my head slightly when I open them again. She's still there, still bewitching, but she's not mine anymore.

Dee drops her hands and steps back. Whatever she sees in my face causes her to cringe away from me. My mom glares at me and places an arm around Dee's shoulders. They go into the room, but I hang back for a moment to get my heart under control and remind myself that she can't be trusted.

Sucking in a deep breath, I enter the room. Laying on the bed is a small boy. His eyes are closed, and from the doorway, I can tell he's way too thin. Even his color is a little off. He's far too pale. Mom and Diandra are on one side of the bed, so I walk around to the other. His little face is relaxed in sleep, and his mouth is open. Mom is right, he's the spitting image of me at his age. Reaching out, I brush the top of his head. He doesn't stir, but his mouth closes.

"He's had a big day," whispers Dee.

Clutched in his arms is a teddy bear. The boy looks so sweet, and my heart breaks a little at my attitude toward his mother.

"What do you need me to do?" I ask in a voice that's barely above a whisper.

"What do you need *us* to do?" my mother corrects me.

"His doctor will want to see you. If you'll follow me, I'll see if he's in his office."

Not able to stop myself, I reach out again and touch his head. I need to reassure myself he's real.

I nod once at him, then say, "Be back soon."

His face scrunches up, and I think he's going to wake, but in the blink of an eye, he goes back to his relaxed pose. Smiling, I meet Dee and my mom in the hallway.

Dee smiles at me, and I quickly lose the smile on my face. I'm mad as hell at her, and I'm not going to give her an inch. At my sudden change of expression, Dee also loses her smile and gestures for us to follow her.

She has obviously spent a good deal of time here. Not only do the staff know her name, but she knows theirs. Eventually, we come to an office, and Dee walks right in. A woman is behind a desk on the phone, and she points at a door, nodding for Dee to go in.

Dee knocks once and then opens it. An older gentleman is standing on the other side of the room, putting on a white lab coat.

"Dr. Otto, this is Grayson and Minerva Moore. Gray is Dawson's dad."

The doctor finishes putting on his coat and walks toward us, a huge smile on his face. "Well, I'll be! You're Grayson

Moore of the New England Warriors! You boys did good." He takes my hand and pumps it up and down.

"Yes, sir, we did."

Dr. Otto looks at Diandra. "I know you said that your son's father was a professional athlete, but I had no idea it would be Grayson Moore."

Diandra smiles. "I told you who he was."

Dr. Otto lets go of my hand and nods. "You did, but..."

Diandra rolls her eyes. "Yes, I did. Could you please explain to Gray and his mom what we need them to do."

"Of course, sit, sit!" orders the doctor.

"What do you need us to do?" I ask as my mother takes a seat. I decide to remain standing.

"We'll need a urine test and a blood test. The blood test will see if you have a matching blood type and antigens. The only other thing we need to consider is your overall health, but looking at you, I can't see that being a problem." His gaze goes to mom. "Unfortunately, Mrs. Moore, you're too old to be a donor."

Mom's face falls, but she quickly recovers. "How soon can he do this?" asks my mother, gesturing toward me.

"Now, if you'd like?" replies the doctor.

Mom nods at him, and I lock eyes with Dee. Her blue eyes that I remember so clearly as being full of life are now cloudy with fear and stress. She's watching me as her hands nervously twitch at her sides.

"I'm good to go."

Dee visibly relaxes. "Thank you."

I nod at her, then put my attention back on the doctor. Being in the same room and looking at her stirs up all those old emotions that I long ago buried.

"Come on, Doc, lead the way."

He walks out of his office and stops so I can walk beside him. "So, tell me, what's Colton Anders like in real life?"

I grin at him. "Colt is my best friend. Between you and me, Doc, he's a pain in the ass but an exceptional football player."

"I noticed earlier in the season he wasn't playing to his full potential, but he sure seems to have sorted himself out for the last few games."

"You need to have your head in the right space. Football isn't all brawn. You've got to see the goal and go for it."

"Still working your plan, are you, Gray?" asks Dee.

"My plan?"

"Yes, when I knew you, you had a five-year plan. Is it all working out?"

There's an edge to her voice that wasn't there before.

I frown at her. "Not everything went to plan." I stare straight ahead. "But you, of course, know that."

Her sharp intake of breath lets me know that she understands my meaning. It might make me an insensitive bastard, but I hope my little barb hurt her.

CHAPTER 13

GRAYSON

The test results will take a week, and because I want to hurt Dee, I also asked for a paternity test. My mother hasn't spoken to me since we've left the hospital. We're staying at Dee's apartment. It overlooks the park. On the ride up in the elevator, it's obvious that she's doing better than I thought. I should've known she'd succeed. Dee was always driven to be the best.

The elevator stops, and Dee walks out first.

She points to a door on her left. "The kitchen is through there." Dee continues walking. "I thought you might want to freshen up, Minerva."

The floors are marble, and Mom's and Dee's shoes make click-clacking noises on its surface as they walk down the hallway.

"I had this room made up for you. It's normally used as a library, but it has its own bathroom, although it is kind of small."

She opens the door, and we all walk in. There's a four-poster bed in the middle of the room. The floors in here are wooden with a herringbone pattern.

"This is small?" Mom asks.

"Oh. Not the room, the bathroom. It's through there," replies Dee as she points to a closed door.

"It'll be fine, honey," assures Mom.

"Gray, if you'll follow me?"

I put Mom's small carry-on on the bed. "Are you okay, Mom?"

"I'm fine. I might just have a little lie-down."

"Yell if you need me."

Mom goes up on her tiptoes to kiss my cheek and whispers, "Be nice."

I nod at her once, then follow Dee back out into the hallway. She walks toward the elevator and then takes the first door on her left. It opens into another hallway with three doors along it.

Dee opens the first door. "This is your room."

The room has massive windows, which would let the light pour in, and a door on either side.

"That door is the door to your mother's bathroom and that one," she points at the opposite door. "Is the bathroom that connects to Dawson's room. Not that he's using it right now, so you may as well."

"How big is this place?"

Dee waves her hand in the air. "I don't use all of it. My room is on the other side of Dawson's. When he's home, we use our bedrooms, the kitchen, and one of the living rooms."

"One of?"

Dee shrugs. "Like I said, we don't use all of the rooms."

"Do you rent?"

Dee shuffles from foot to foot, looking uncomfortable. "Sort of. This belongs to a friend."

I drop my bag, and it makes a thud as it hits the wooden floor.

"Would you like to see Dawson's room?"

I nod. The need to see his room is overwhelming me, not that I'll admit it to Dee or my mother.

Dee goes back out into the hallway. "The room at the end of the hall is mine."

She opens the next door, and we both walk in. It's a blue room, and someone has painted clouds on the ceiling. The room is full of toys, and on one wall is a giant photograph of me in my New England Warrior's uniform. I'm not smiling, I look angry, and it's not a picture I recognize.

"Where did you get that?"

"A friend."

"Does it scare him?"

"Dawson?" Dee laughs. "No. Sometimes I come in here, and he's pulling faces trying to copy your pose. He loves to watch you play."

As I walk around the room, I notice there's an overabundance of New England Warrior memorabilia. I might not have known that Dawson existed, but it's pretty evident he knows exactly who I am. Next to his bed is a photograph of Dee and me taken way back when I thought she'd be in my life forever. We're both smiling, and we looked happy. In retrospect, I'll be in her life forever now that we have a child to bind us.

I pick up the picture in its plain wooden frame and turn it toward Dee. "Happier times, huh?"

Dee nods. "I thought it was important for him to know who his father is." Her eyes sparkle with unshed tears.

Part of me wants to comfort her and tell her it will be okay, but there's still a part of me that's raw and bloody from the way she left things. And right now, that part is winning. I put the picture down and continue to walk around his room.

"He has a lot of stuff."

"Mom and Dad spoil him."

I nod and open the door to the other bathroom. It's has a door into Dee's room which is open.

"You share a bathroom?"

"No, I have my own." Dee pushes past me into the bathroom and shuts the other door. "I leave both doors open when Dawson is home, in case he needs me."

"Diandra! Are you here?" yells a male voice.

Dee visibly pales as she looks at me. "Please, don't be mad, Gray. It's not what you think."

Tyson Reed walks into the room. "Ah, Grayson, you're here. I hope everything is to your liking?"

My head twists back and forth between Dee and the owner of the New England Warriors. I'm speechless as I piece it together in my mind.

This apartment.

The private hospital.

The New England Warriors memorabilia.

Dee and Tyson are a couple.

I'm such an idiot.

Cracking my head from side to side, I nod at him. "Yeah. Everything is peachy keen."

Looking at Dee, I shake my head slightly and walk through the other bathroom and into my room without a backward glance.

CHAPTER 14

DIANDRA

As soon as I heard Tyson's voice, I knew how Gray would react. The shake of his head, the way he clamped his mouth shut, and then the look of disgust he gave me as he strode out of the room.

When he closed both doors to the other bathroom, I nearly screamed. Instead, I walked up to Tyson and gave him a scathing look.

"What?" he asks.

"What?" I move into his personal space. "What?" I ask again, in a higher octave, as I throw my arms in the air. "He doesn't know about you!" I hiss.

"Oh."

"Oh?" I'm so angry I could slap him. "He hasn't agreed to help Dawson. He's only just had the fucking tests done to see if he's a match. What if he is, and now he won't help? Jesus, Tyson!" Tears spill down my cheeks.

"I didn't know you hadn't told him." Tyson reaches out and puts his hands on my shoulders. "You *were* going to tell him?"

"Of course I was."

The tears won't stop, and Tyson pulls me in for a hug as I continue to cry. "I'll explain it to him." He strokes up and down my back. "Please don't cry."

I push back from him, wiping at my face as I do. "No, it has to be me."

"What do you want me to do?"

Tyson has been my greatest friend and ally through this entire ordeal. He loves Dawson just as much as I do.

"Could you stay on your side of the apartment until I've talked to Gray?"

Hurt flashes across his face, but he nods once and leaves the room. I know I've hurt him deeply. But I've always been honest with him, and I love Tyson like a brother. There are no romantic feelings for him at all.

I walk into my room and to my dressing table. Staring at myself in the mirror, I see circles under my eyes. Using a little foundation, I try to cover them up and apply a fresh coat of lipstick, then I drag a brush through my hair. Feeling a little better about myself, I go in search of Gray. Nervously, I stand outside his door. I raise my hand to knock just as he pulls it open.

He's got his bag in his hand.

Damn! It looks like he's going to leave.

Putting my hand on his chest, I push him back into the room, then I bend and take his bag off him and put it on a chair. Gray doesn't speak. I put my hand in his and tug him to the leather couch at the end of his bed. We both sit. Gray is staring at me, his nostrils flared, and I know he's angry.

Folding my hands in my lap, I take a deep breath and gaze into his deep brown eyes. "This is Tyson's apartment. He helped me move to New York, and he lets Dawson and I live here."

Gray shakes his head, mouth firmly closed. I wait for him to speak, but he doesn't.

"I'm not with Tyson, nor have I ever been romantically involved with him." Swallowing, the sound seems very loud to my ears. "Gray, we weren't ready for a child. You told me a child would ruin everything. You'd just been signed, and you were happy. I didn't want to complicate things for you. I didn't want you to have to choose."

Gray takes a breath, and I watch his chest go up and down. His hands are clenched into fists as he listens to me talk. He breaks eye contact with me and shakes his head once. "You should've told me."

"I'm sorry."

"You were everything to me. I'd have moved heaven and earth to make you happy. Why didn't you trust me, Dee?"

Reaching out, I put one of my hands over one of his fists. "You had a five-year plan. Having a pregnant girlfriend wasn't part of your plan, and I did try to talk to you, Gray, but you said a child would ruin everything."

His eyes come back to mine. "And Tyson Reed? Did he simply replace me?"

Snatching my hand back, I sit a little straighter. "No. No one has ever taken your place."

Gray's head tilts to the side as he searches my face. "I don't believe you. No man does what Tyson has done if he's not getting a little something in return."

I stand, staggering back a few steps from him. This isn't the Grayson Moore I once loved. This is some replica of him that only sees lies and deceit.

"Believe what you will. Tyson did have a reason for helping me. He'd just signed you and Colton. You two are now the most valuable players on his team, and if nothing else, Tyson is ruthless. He wanted to win the Super Bowl, and you two helped him do that."

Turning, I stalk out of the room, slamming the door as hard as I can before I run to my bedroom and curl up on my bed and cry.

CHAPTER 15

GRAYSON

When she stumbled away from me, I knew I'd hurt her deeply. Dee's face fell at my accusation. How do I stop myself from wanting to wound her as much as she's wounded me? It feels like she moved to New York, got on with her life, and forgot all about me.

A knock behind me draws my attention, and my mother is standing at the open bathroom door.

"Go after her."

I shake my head.

"I swear, Grayson, if you don't, you'll regret it."

Shaking my head again, I say, "I regret meeting her. I wish I never had."

"Oh, Gray. You loved her once, and that love produced Dawson. He needs you."

"I know, Mom. I'm not walking away from my responsibilities." Standing to face her, I meet her gaze. "See, that's the thing, Mom, I wouldn't have cared about a baby. I'd have married her. Hell, I was *going* to marry her."

Mom lifts her chin. "Diandra is right about a few things."

"Mom," I warn.

She walks toward me, her hands held high. "You listen to me, son. All you ever talked about was your five-year plan. You had your entire life mapped out. The poor girl was scared, and it sounds like she did all of this for *you*. So *you* wouldn't have to choose."

"I'd have chosen her."

"That first year you lived at the stadium. You trained nonstop. All of your focus was on the team, and look where it's got you." Mom puts her hands in mine. "Your team won the Super Bowl." She squeezes my fingers. "If you'd had a child, maybe you wouldn't have been so focused. Maybe you wouldn't be where you are today, but all of this is moot. The reason we're here is for Dawson. Not for you, not for Diandra, and certainly not for the New England Warriors. Being a parent means you put your child first. Diandra has been doing that for three years, and now it's your turn."

Mom's words ring true, except I'd have liked the choice to be in Dawson's life or not. Instead, Dee took that away from me. Now, he's sick and might not survive, so if he is my son, she's robbed me of his life, and that's something I can't get back.

I'm sitting with Mom and Diandra in Dr. Otto's office. Today's the day we find out if I'm a match for Dawson. Mom fidgets in her seat, fussing with the cuff of her jacket. She's more nervous than I am. The doctor is running late, and none of us are talking to each other. The silence is weighing heavily on me, and I know I need to break it, but I'm so angry, hurt, and confused. I'm worried if I open my mouth to speak, I'll only hurt Diandra further.

Mom reaches across me to touch Dee on the leg. "I'm sure everything is going to be fine."

"I hope so. If Gray isn't a match, I'm not sure how long Dawson—" Dee stops talking, her face flushes red, and it looks likes she's on the brink of breaking down.

"We don't know anything yet. Calm down. Let's hear what the doctor has to say."

Dee nods, sucks in a lung full of air, and slowly releases it. Then, she sits next to me, placing her hand on top of mine. I'm not comfortable sitting with her like this, so I slowly extract my hand from hers and stare straight ahead. Three years ago, she left me with no explanation, and I'm not willing to forgive her. Just yet.

Dr. Otto comes in, wearing a smile on his face. "Hello!" He taps away on his computer and swivels the monitor around for us to view.

"Is it good news, Doc?" I ask.

"Very. You are a blood and tissue match, the paternity test came back, and you're a ninety-nine percent match. There's no doubt in my mind that Dawson is your son."

I suck in a breath, blow out my cheeks, and slowly release it. Standing, I nod repeatedly at this news. In my heart, I knew he was mine the moment I laid eyes on him, but a part of me wanted to deny it. Hearing the doctor say the words out loud that he's mine strikes a nerve deep within me.

"Gray?" asks Dee.

I don't look at her. Instead, I focus on the doctor. "What's the next step?"

"I've reviewed your medical file that was sent over from the New England Warriors. It's quite extensive."

"They pay us a lot of money and expect us to be in tip-top condition. Their testing can be rigorous and exhausting, but at least we all know we're fit and good to play."

"I see no reason to delay. We could schedule the procedure for as early as tomorrow."

Dee laughs and claps her hand. "Thank you, Doctor."

Dr. Otto looks from Dee to me, and a small frown creases his forehead. "If you don't mind, I'd like some time alone with Mr. Moore."

Mom and Dee stand, then embrace each other.

"Of course!" beams Mom as she and Dee leave the room, chatting excitedly with each other.

Dr. Otto extends his hand and says, "Please sit, Mr. Moore."

"Call me Gray."

"Gray." He picks up a pen and twirls it between two fingers. "Have you researched this procedure at all?"

"No, sir."

He nods, puts the pen down, and leans forward. "We'll make a small incision below your belly button to remove the kidney."

"Okay, sign me up."

His lips turn down, and his expression turns serious. "It would mean the end of your football career."

I rock back in the chair and shake my head. "What?"

"If you were on a baseball team, we wouldn't be having this conversation, but you're in a high-contact sport. There's a chance you could damage your remaining kidney."

I'm staring at him, completely dumbfounded. My mind has gone into a fog, and I have no idea how to respond.

Dr. Otto sits back. "If you decide to go through with the surgery, you'll remain in the hospital for four to six days, and your recovery time will be approximately six weeks. No heavy lifting. You may experience some tenderness and itching as you heal."

"Wait, wait, wait." I hold up a hand. "No more football?"

"I'm afraid not."

"But that's my job, it's my life. *It is all I have.*"

"It's a sacrifice you'll have to make *if* you go through with the surgery."

"And if I don't go through with it, what will happen to Dawson?"

Dr. Otto's lips turn down, and he shakes his head. "Without a transplant, he will die."

I'm staring at him, my mouth ajar, trying to comprehend everything he's just said. Dr. Otto stands and walks around his desk. He leans against it and crosses his ankles. "Right now, Dawson is doing okay. You have time to think about it."

Sharply I look up at him. "Give me the day. I'll come back tomorrow with an answer. I need to think."

He reaches out and pats my shoulder. "Of course. Take all the time you need."

Standing, I walk out of the room and head toward Dawson's room. I haven't met him yet. He's been asleep the few times I have been here, and I've been reluctant to wake him. Part of me doesn't want to form a bond with him. Part of me thinks of him as only Diandra's son, not mine.

Entering his room, he's awake. He's got a small doll of me, and he's attacking his teddy bear with it. I'm guessing both of them came from Tyson Reed. My mouth turns down at the thought of him. He's remained scarce since we've arrived, apart from that one meeting in Dawson's room.

Dawson looks up and sees me, and a smile splits his face. "Grayson Moore!"

"Better known as your dad," I reply.

Dawson nods. "I knew that!"

I ruffle his hair and sit on the bed near him. "How are you feeling?"

"I'm okay, not as tired today."

"Where's your momma?"

He shrugs and looks down as he plays with the figurine of me.

"She won't be far away."

He looks at me from underneath his lashes. "Are you going to stay?"

"Football season is over, and I have nowhere else I'd rather be."

He drops the toy and grabs my hand. "I watch you on TV."

"You like football?" He nods. "Maybe you and I could go to a game sometime?"

His smile gets bigger, and he nods. "Yes!"

"Have you ever been to a game, little man?"

"That's what Momma calls me." He falls back onto his pillows. "Momma won't take me to a game."

"Well, we'll have to talk to her about it."

The boy holds up my hand and puts his small palm against mine. This innocent act melts my heart. Staring at his small hand on my large one, something inside me breaks.

"Momma says one day I'm going to grow up big and strong like you."

"For sure, little man."

He yawns and rubs his eyes.

"Are you tired?"

Dawson shakes his head.

"You sure?"

He nods.

"You know it's okay to have a nap. I have them all the time."

"You do?"

"Oh, yeah. You can't play football without rest."

He closes his eyes and then opens them suddenly. "You'll be here when I wake up?"

"If I'm not, you get your momma to ring me, and I'll come right back."

"Okay."

His eyes close, and I wait until he's dropped off before I leave the room. Pulling my cell phone out of my pocket, I dial Colt.

"Hey, Gray, how are things?"

"Messy."

I close my eyes and lean against the wall out in the hallway.

"How can I help?"

It's so like Colt to do that. He's a good guy, and I'm lucky to have met him.

"I don't know that you can."

"Need me to come?"

"Yeah, man, that'd be good."

"I'll book a flight. See you soon, brother."

The line goes dead. He is more than my best friend, he's family.

If anyone can help me through this mess, it'll be Colton Anders.

CHAPTER 16

GRAYSON

I've avoided both my mother and Diandra. They've called my cell phone multiple times, but I let it go to voicemail. Before I can talk to either of them, I need to decide what I'm going to do. I'm waiting in the bar at The Langham Hotel for Colt. He hasn't checked in yet, but he shouldn't be far away. His flight landed forty minutes ago.

"Excuse me, are you Grayson Moore?" Turning slightly, I come face to face with a blonde bombshell. "You *are* Grayson Moore!"

Nodding and grinning at her, I stand and hold out my hand. "Yes, ma'am, I'm Grayson Moore, but my friends call me Gray."

"Oh, I can't believe it! I'm a huge fan. Congratulations on the Super Bowl!" She throws her arms around me for an instant, then moves back. "You *have* to let me buy you a drink."

I pick up my full glass and wave it in front of her. "I've got one, but I could get you a drink?"

She pretends to look embarrassed and puts her hand on my arm. "Well, that would be fabulous." The bombshell positions herself on the chair next to mine and then holds out her hand. "I'm Tiffany."

I shake her hand and then sit back down. "Nice to meet you, Tiffany."

"What *are you* doing in New York?"

"I have family here, and the season is over."

"Ahh, time to relax and party."

I've met women like her hundreds of times. They're fans looking to add my name to their bedpost, and normally, I'm polite and send them on their way, but I can use the distraction right now.

"Something like that. How about you? Do you live in New York?"

I signal for the bartender to come over.

"Yes, lived here all my life. I'm meeting a client for a drink."

"What can I get you?" asks the bartender.

"Whiskey, neat," replies Tiffany.

"Damn, girl! You sure you can handle the heat?" I tease.

Tiffany smiles and pushes her hair off one shoulder. "Nothing like a little liquid courage to sharpen the senses."

The bartender puts a drink in front of her, and she picks it up.

"To new friends."

We clink glasses and sip our drinks.

A hand lands on my shoulder, and I turn to find Colt standing there. Instantly, I get off my seat and pull him in for a hug.

"I sure am glad you're here."

Colt looks past me to Tiffany. "You sure about that?"

"Colt, this is Tiffany... Tiffany, this is Colt."

She slides off the bar stool and puts both her hands around Colt's extended one.

"Well, hell, today's my lucky day! Not one New England Warrior but two, and the quarterback, no less!"

Colt smiles at her, and I swear she melts on the spot. "Nice to meet you, Tiffany."

He tries to extract his hand, but she hangs on.

"The pleasure is all mine," she gushes.

Colt smiles, then looks down at his hand, she blushes, and lets him go.

"Sorry to break this up, but I need to have a sit-down with my friend here. It was nice meeting you," says Colt to Tiffany.

"Oh! But he hasn't finished his drink yet," pouts Tiffany.

"He'll live," replies Colt as he leads me away.

Tiffany doesn't look happy, but she rearranges herself back on the chair, and Colt drags me through the hotel to the elevators.

"What the hell was that?"

"Tiffany," I reply with a shrug.

"More like a football bunny. You don't do football bunnies... that's my area."

"No, it used to be your area. Now, you've got Skye, and you're all partied out."

"Hardly. Have you seen how much my woman can drink? And I swear she can eat more than me too. She's already gone upstairs to check out our room."

Colt is smiling as he talks about Skye. Until her, he was a manwhore. No nicer way to say it. He fooled around with anything in a skirt. Skye was the first woman who rejected him, and his ego couldn't handle it, so he chased her like he's never chased a woman before. By the time he caught her, he was hooked.

The elevator opens, and he walks to his room, opening the door. "So wanna tell me what the issue is?"

"You mean apart from me having a son I didn't know about?"

Colt flops into a chair and nods. "Yeah, apart from that. What's he like?"

I sit down on the couch and look at him. "Sick. He's so small. He weighs nothing."

"What's his name again?"

"Dawson. Dee named him after my grandfather. All he does is sleep."

Skye walks into the room from the bedroom. "Hey, boys." She kisses Colt on the lips, then sits next to me on the couch.

"How are you doing, Gray?"

"I'm fine," I automatically reply.

Skye and Colt exchange a glance, then she stands. "I'm going shopping. Can I get either of you anything?"

"I'm good."

"Do you need money, babe? Take my credit card in my wallet in that bag." Colt points to a bag near the door to the bedroom."

"Pfft! As if I need you to buy things for me, Colton Anders. My word." Skye leans down and kisses him again. "I'll be an hour. Call me if you need anything."

"Have you got a room key?"

Skye holds one up as she walks out.

"You got lucky with her."

"Don't I know it." Colt grins at me. "You want a drink?"

"Water?"

Colt stands and opens the mini-refrigerator and throws a bottle at me. I catch it in one hand.

"Show off. Next, you'll be wanting my position on the team."

I shake my head and put my elbows on my knees and lean forward. "Dawson needs a kidney transplant. His odds of surviving are..." I search for the right words, then shrug as nothing comes. "He'll die if he doesn't get one."

"Are you a match?"

"Did Dee tell you?"

"Dee said he was sick and that you were the only one who might be able to help him, so I figured it was something like that."

"I'm a match."

Colt frowns at me. "That's a good thing, right? You can give him one of yours?"

I nod, open the bottle, and take a swig of water.

"Brother, what's going on?"

"It's messed up. Did you know Tyson Reed helped Dee move here? She lives in his apartment."

"The owner of our team, Tyson Reed?"

"Yeah, the one and the very same."

"Why would he do that?"

I shrug. It's another thing I've been avoiding. "I don't know, I haven't asked him."

Colt looks thoughtful. "Are you going to give Dawson one of your kidneys?"

"Yes." Then I shake my head. "No." I sigh. "I don't know."

Colt quirks an eyebrow. "What's going on."

Leaning back, I put one arm out over the top of the couch. "If I go through with it, I won't be able to play football anymore. Apparently, there's too much risk of getting hurt with only one kidney."

Colt's mouth drops open, and he makes a strange noise. "You won't be able to play?"

I shake my head. "I've probably only got three more years in me. But I was hoping to solidify some sponsorship deals in the meantime."

Colt nods. "I'm about the same. My shoulder kills me, now." Subconsciously, he touches his shoulder and rubs. "You beat the average. Did you know the average life span for a football linebacker is three and a half years and quarterbacks only last three?"

"Yeah, but then you've got guys like Brett Favre who lasted forever. You might be like him."

Colt shakes his head. "I've done well these past three years, but my body is hurting. We both know that most quarterbacks start to get down-traded at the four-year mark as our injuries catch up with us."

Both of us are silent as we think about our career paths.

Colt clears his throat. "What are you going to do?"

"I've got deals in the fire, but I needed to last at least two more years." Colt locks eyes with me. "I love the game. It's earned me a lot of money. Not as much as you, Mr. Quarterback."

Colt smiles. "Yeah, but you were always better with money than me."

"And if it weren't for you, I wouldn't have gotten a Nike or Gatorade sponsorship deal."

"You forgot Calvin Klein," teases Colt. "Seriously, though, you always said you'd go into sports medicine and work for one of the teams."

"I know, I just thought I had more time."

"What does Diandra say?"

I put my hands in my lap. "I haven't spoken to her about it."

"Why not?"

"It's hard to be in the same room as her. I'm angry and hurt. Worse, I'm a complete bastard to her."

Colt frowns. "That's not like you, brother."

"She's the only woman I've ever loved. The way she left, it gutted me."

Colt tilts his head to the side. "I have an idea."

His eyes sparkle at his newfound plan. Colt's ideas always involve women and drinking, so I groan at him and shake my head.

"No."

"Hear me out."

"No," I repeat.

Colt waves a hand at me, pulls out his cell phone, and texts someone. "I have a friend in town. Lochlan MacKenny. He's a model with one of the bigger agencies here in New York. He's only got his hand in a lot of real estate deals. We're going to meet up with him tonight, so bring Dee. We can make a night of it. It'll give you a chance to escape the complexities of your situation, and you can both relax in an easy-going I'm-here-to-have-fun kind of way."

"I don't know."

"When was the last time you let your hair down?"

"The night we won the Super Bowl."

"That doesn't count."

Looking up at the ceiling, I shake my head. "I don't remember."

"Exactly! All you do is train. When was the last time you had fun?"

"I don't think Dee will come."

"I'll ask her." Colt types away on his cell phone again. "Done."

"How do you have Dee's number?"

"I asked her for it."

"Right. Of course, you did."

His phone chimes, and he smiles as he reads the text. "Lochlan is a yes, except he'll be flying solo. That's kinda weird for him." Colt's phone chimes again, and he grins as he waves the screen in my direction. "A-ha! She said yes. I've booked a restaurant for six, all I need to do is let them know there's now five of us, and we're all set."

I look at the clock on the wall. "It's five now."

"Well, you better get going. I'll text you the address."

"Colt, I'm not so sure this is a good idea."

"It's a great idea. You can meet Lochlan and see if he has any connections in the modeling arena, and you can see if he has any deals going in his real estate business. He's making a killing at the moment. Well, he says he is, so we can pump him for information." Colt nods to himself as he stands and walks toward the bedroom.

"I guess I'll go?"

Colt stops and looks at me. "Yep. Wear something nice. Maybe get Dee some flowers?"

I stand and shake my head. "This *isn't* a date."

"Sure it is." He laughs. "And Gray?"

I stop and turn around. "Yes?"

"We both know you aren't going to let Dawson die. You need to get right with it up here." Colt taps the side of his head.

I know he's right, but I still have plans for myself where football is concerned.

Can I really give it up and go in another direction?

But Colt is right, I can't let my son die.

CHAPTER 17

DIANDRA

I'm in my bedroom getting ready. It doesn't leave me much time to primp and preen with only an hour to get to the restaurant. It surprised me to get the invitation from Colton. When I left Gray, I left him too. He was a lot of fun to hang out with, but he was Gray's best friend, so I knew I couldn't continue our friendship. It would've been impossible. Sitting on the end of my bed, I'm slipping on heels when there's a knock on my door. Looking up, Tyson is there.

"Do I need to wave a white flag?" He pulls a sock out of his pocket and waves it in front of himself.

Laughing, I wave a hand at him. "I hope that's clean."

He sniffs it and chokes. "Yep." He coughs a couple of times and puts it back in his pocket. "You look nice. Are you going out?"

Tyson comes and sits next to me on the bed.

"Colton Anders is in town with his girlfriend, and they've invited me to dinner."

Tyson raises his eyebrows. "*Okay*. Same girlfriend he has in Boston?"

Understanding his meaning, I nod. "Yes. He's changed a lot, hasn't he?"

"I'll say. I've been waiting for the lawsuits with that one. *So* many women. I'm surprised he doesn't have paternity suits piled up to his ears." Tyson closes his eyes and shakes his head. "Sorry, that was thoughtless. Sometimes I forget."

Patting his leg, I stand and walk over to my dressing table and put on a pair of earrings. "It's fine, I knew you didn't mean anything by it." I stare at him in the mirror. "I've known Colt a long time, and I remember what he was like."

"Dr. Otto told me the good news."

Turning around, I smile at him. "It *is* good news."

"You look happy. It's been a long time since I've seen that smile, and it's good that you're going out. Although, I did notice you put Minerva in charge of Dawson. You could've asked me. I would have stayed with him."

"Minerva is family." Tyson's face falls, and I shake my head. "Sorry, that's not what I meant."

Tyson stands and walks toward the door. "It's fine. Have an enjoyable night, you deserve it."

I jog to catch up with him in the hallway, grabbing him by the arm. "Tyson, please don't be upset. I simply meant she's his grandmother. You *are* family, you're Dawson's godfather, and he loves you. *I* love you."

"But you're not *in love* with me, are you?" He reaches up to touch my face, and his expression looks pained.

"No. You know I'd do *anything* for you. But I think of you as a brother, not that way."

Tyson nods and smiles down at me. "Yeah. You're still hung up on Grayson, aren't you?"

I shake my head. "I thought I was. But he's not the man I fell in love with. Something is missing in his personality now. Gray was never cold or distant. I don't think he's spent any time alone with Dawson. He's just here because he thinks he has to be. Gray is doing what he believes is right. Now that he knows Dawson is his, he's only fulfilling his fatherly duties."

"I've seen the way he stares at you. The man still has feelings for you."

I purse my lips together and shake my head. "We can agree to disagree on that one."

"Do you need a lift?"

"Yes, please. I'm going to be a bit late."

I run back into my room, pick up my clutch, and jog back to him. "How do I look?"

"Stunning, as always."

Tyson walks out into the foyer and holds out his arm. I giggle, link my arm with his, and we go down in the elevator to the garage.

CHAPTER 18

GRAYSON

Like a peeping tom, I listened to Diandra and Tyson Reed outside my bedroom door. Part of me believed they were a couple, but after that exchange, I know they aren't. I wait until I hear the elevator descend before leaving my room. She's not in love with him, but he's my son's godfather. Something else I didn't know.

I pull my cell phone out of my pocket and dial Colt. He answers on the third ring.

"Where are you? Still doing your hair?"

"You know you think you're funny, but you are not, and my hair is perfect," I quip. Colton barks out a laugh. "I'm going to be a little late. And I noticed the restaurant is the one in your hotel. You could've told me."

"I wanted it to be a surprise." Laughs Colt.

"I could have just stayed there and walked downstairs."

"Yeah, you could have, but I wanted you to look nice for Diandra."

"The Diandra who doesn't know I'm coming tonight... that Diandra?"

Colt goes quiet.

"Colt?"

"She wouldn't have come if she'd known you were. This is my way of trying to fix things. Get your ass over here." He hangs up, and I shake my head at my cell phone. So like him to try to make things better for me.

The elevator comes back up, and I get in and go down to the lobby. Fred, the doorman, is there.

"Hello, Fred."

"Hello, Mr. Moore. How are things?"

"Good, Fred. Do you think you could hail me a cab?"

"Sure can. Where are you off to?"

"The Langham Hotel."

"You leaving us?"

I shake my head. "No, I'm going there for dinner with friends. Colton Anders."

"You two are always as thick as thieves in the tabloids. Are any more of your teammates going to be there?"

"No. Just us."

"Well, you have a good night."

Fred walks out onto the sidewalk with me following him. He hails the cab and lets the cabbie know where we're going. I wave him goodnight, and thankfully, the cab driver gets me there with minimal conversation.

If I weren't strapped for time, I'd have walked. It should take about fifty minutes to walk there but only twelve minutes by cab. Well, depending on traffic. Thankfully, the cabbie gets me to the hotel at six seventeen. I pay him and jog inside. The restaurant is on the second floor.

As I walk in, Dee is sitting next to Skye, and on her other side must be Lochlan MacKenny. He has his arm on the back of Dee's chair, and he's leaning in as he talks to the ladies. Colt looks a little uncomfortable, and his demeanor worsens when his eyes land on me.

I approach the table, and Dee glances up and then does a double-take as I stand in front of them all. Colt immediately stands and holds out his hand.

"Gray! So good to see you."

I shake his hand and smile. It obvious he still hasn't told Dee I'm joining them.

"Hey, Colt, Skye, imagine you two being here?" I fake a smile and raise my eyebrows at Dee.

"Please, join us," gushes Skye.

"Don't mind if I do." I sit opposite Dee.

"Hello, I'm Lochlan, and this is Dee."

I shake his hand and laugh. "Hey, Lochlan, and yes, I know Dee, she's the mother of my child."

Lochlan's smile falters, and he looks directly at Colt. "Right. Sorry, shall we trade places?"

Dee reaches out and touches Lochlan's upper arm. "It was a long time ago. We aren't together anymore."

Lochlan lets go of my hand and smiles at her. "Good to know."

"Oh, I don't know, Dee, it wasn't *that* long ago," interjects Colt.

Dee looks shocked for a moment, then regains her composure. "Well, the point is we aren't together anymore." She looks at me. "Are we, Gray?"

"No. We're not. You're good sitting where you are." I gesture toward Colt. "Colt tells me you're a model and real estate mogul. It looks like my pro-ball career is over, so I was hoping you could give me some tips?"

Skye chokes on her wine, Colt hits her on the back, and Diandra's mouth is wide open.

"What?" she asks in almost a shriek.

Poor Lochlan looks confused.

"Skye, are you okay?" asks Colt as she continues to cough.

Skye can only nod as she tries to bring herself under control.

"Once I donate a kidney, that's it. No more football for me."

Dee stands. "No, no, no! This isn't what I wanted."

I stand. "Well, it's not about you. It's about what's best for Dawson."

Tear spring to her eyes, and she shakes her head, then she looks down at Lochlan. "It was so nice meeting you." Then she turns slightly to face a still coughing Skye. "And you too."

Dee picks up her clutch and stalks toward the elevators without a backward glance.

"If you don't go after her, I'm going to knock you into next week," states Colt.

Skye nods furiously next to him.

"Gray, I don't know you, but I do know that's one hell of a woman, and if you don't chase after her, I will," says Lochlan.

Blowing out my cheeks, I do an about-turn and run after her. Dee is furiously pressing the button for the elevator. As I get to her, the doors open, and she walks inside with me right behind her. The doors close, Dee wraps her arms around herself and turns around. Her eyes go wide.

"Leave me alone, Gray."

I shake my head and close the gap between us. Dee walks backward until her body hits the back of the elevator, but I keep coming. I put a hand on either side of her head, and she looks up at me like a rabbit caught in a trap.

"Back up, Gray!"

I shake my head. "Talk to me."

"You're too close. Step back."

"Not until you talk to me."

A tear slides down her cheek, and I brush it away with my thumb, keeping my hand pressed to her face. "Please, don't cry."

Dee stands straighter, her head pressed up against the elevator wall. "Step. Back."

I take in a deep breath, and her perfume fills my nostrils. My other hand moves to cup the other side of her face, and I move in, my lips a whisper from hers. Dee's eyes go to my mouth, and then I crush her lips to mine. She whimpers, but she doesn't push me back.

As I deepen the kiss, her hands clutch at my shirt. One of my hands moves down her body to her waist, and I press her closer to me. Dee's mouth opens, an invitation for me to explore what was once mine.

The doors to the elevator open, and people come in, but neither of us stop. It feels like an eternity since I've felt this way. Like a man dying for a drink, I want more. This kiss isn't enough. I want all of her.

Someone clears their throat, and Dee pulls back, resting her head on my chest.

"Maybe you two should get a room?" suggests a female voice full of mirth.

I put my hand in Dee's, and as soon as the doors open again, pull her with me. Thankfully, we're in the hotel lobby. My only thought is to get Dee alone, so I drag her toward a cab and push her through the open door.

"Beresford Apartments," I growl at the cabbie.

"You're Grayson Moore."

Jesus, every cab I've gotten into in this city and not one of them has known me, but this guy does. I don't want to make small talk. I want to reconnect with Dee.

"Yes, he is," announces Dee.

"Good job on the Super Bowl. You know I've always been a fan of the New England Warriors. You guys were a shoo-in this year. How do you think you'll go next year?"

Locking eyes with Dee, I say, "They'll win. But this was my last year with them."

"True? I haven't read that in the papers."

"Yeah, I haven't announced it yet. My son is sick, and he needs one of my kidneys, so no more football for me."

"Geez, sorry to hear that about your boy. You'll be missed. You really think the Warriors can do it without you?"

"They'll manage, they still have the best quarterback in the league. Colt won't let them down."

Dee shakes her head. "I won't let you."

"It's not about you, Dee. It's about doing what's right, and helping little man *is* what's right."

A tear slides down her face, then another. "I'm so sorry, Gray."

Grasping her face, I shake my head. "Don't be. Sometimes life throws you a curveball, and you can either tuck and run or face it head-on." I brush her tears away. "I'm not running anymore."

"Ahh, Mr. Moore, Gray?" I turn to face the cabbie and give him an inquiring look. "We're here."

Dee opens the door, and I reluctantly let her go. The cabbie is talking, but I don't hear a word he's saying. I toss him fifty dollars and follow Dee out into the open air. She's shaking her head and muttering to herself as she hurries toward the entry to the Beresford.

I catch up with her at the elevators. "Dee, talk to me."

The doors open, and she walks into the empty space. I hesitate for a moment, then follow her inside. This time I don't crowd her but keep my distance.

Dee turns to stare at me. "This can't go any further."

"Why?"

"This thing between us isn't real. You're remembering a girl who's long since disappeared."

I shake my head. "No, she's still there, she's just grown up, and she's the mother of my son."

Dee shakes her head. The elevator comes to a stop, the doors open, and Tyson Reed is standing there. Anger boils through me. I take two steps toward him, and he staggers back.

"Grayson, let's talk about this."

"You took her away. You kept her and my son here! Did you think you could replace me, Mr. Reed? Did you think becoming godfather to my son would make him think you're his father?"

"Grayson!" yells Diandra as she positions herself in front of him. "It was my idea!"

I look past her to Tyson Reed, who takes another few steps away from us. "Dee, leave me and *Mr.* Reed alone."

Dee shakes her head.

"I give you my word I won't hurt him, but he and I are going to have a sit-down."

"Gray—"

"Now, Dee." I look into her eyes, and in a softer tone, I say, "Go shower. I'll be in, in a minute."

Dee tilts her head, and I think she's going to argue with me, but to my surprise, she nods and disappears down the hallway that leads to her bedroom.

He watches her leave and lets out a sigh. "She's never stopped loving you." He turns his back on me, then stops and waves a hand for me to follow him. "It's about time you called me Tyson and heard the entire story."

I follow him to the end of the hallway, where he turns left and continues on, going past many doors. I knew this place was large, but I had no idea how extensive it is. Finally, Tyson opens a door on his right and walks in. Inside is a library and off to one side is a bar. He walks in behind it and pours two drinks, then comes back to me, offering me one of the glasses.

"I can't."

He frowns, shrugs, and sits on one of the leather couches.

"I need you to know I didn't bring her here to hurt you." He crosses his legs and sips his drink. "Diandra was lost. She told me you didn't want a child, and she couldn't get herself to tell you or to terminate. I was in a position to help her, so I did."

"You love her." It's not a question but a statement.

Tyson nods. "That came later." He sighs. "I don't know when it happened." He looks down at the rug at our feet. "Not long after she moved here. I watched her throughout the pregnancy, I was there for Dawson's birth, and I've looked out for her these past three years." He pauses for a moment. "But through it all, she'd ask me about you. How were you doing? Did I know how your mother was? Should she tell you?"

"And what did you say to that?"

His eyes find mine. "It became obvious she was never going to love me, so I told her she should tell you. But the older Dawson got, the harder it became for her, and eventually, she decided it would be easier not to tell you. I guess the universe has a perverse sense of humor. It's like it made Dawson sick on purpose, so she could find her way back to you."

"That's a shitty way to look at it."

"Yeah, but do you know how rare it is for a child under four to get Goodpasture Syndrome?"

I shake my head.

He grimaces. "The odds are miniscule, something like one in one million people get it every year, and the risk of a child getting is so much more than that." Tyson wags a finger at me. "The universe has plans for you two." He takes a sip of his drink. "Or should I say you three?"

"The operation to remove one of my kidneys will mean the end of my football career."

Tyson's eyes widen, and he laughs. "Wow, the fucking universe just keeps on giving, doesn't it?"

"It's elective surgery."

"Meaning I could keep the rest of the money owed to you in your contract." I nod and purse my lips together. "Would you do that? Give it all up?"

"Yes," I answer without hesitation.

Tyson smiles. "Good."

He takes a sip of his drink, and I realize I'm only going to have the money in my accounts that I have right now. It's a lot of money, but it's not enough to see Dawson and Dee through the medical expenses we're going to face for the rest of his life.

"Of course, I won't do that. I couldn't do it to Dee or Dawson, and I'm going to get some good press out of this. *And* I'm going to use it as a bargaining chip."

"How so?"

His lips turn down. "I'm very fond of Dawson, and I am his godfather." He leans forward and puts down his drink. "I'd very much like to be a part of his life as he grows up if you'll let me." Tyson stands, facing me. "Please don't take him from me. You can have whatever is owed to you regardless, but I'd like you to consider letting me see your son."

Tyson Reed isn't a bad person. He may have conspired to keep Dee and Dawson from me, but he genuinely cares for both of them.

"They'll be moving out of here."

Tyson nods. "Is that a yes?"

I hold out my hand to him, and he puts his hand in mine.

"It's a yes." We shake hands, and he tries to pull out of my grasp. "But no more secrets, Tyson, you're family now. We don't keep secrets."

"Agreed."

I let him go, then walk out of the room and go in search of Dee.

CHAPTER 19

DIANDRA

Leaving those two alone is a bad idea. I know they need to work through their issues, but a part of me would like to be there to referee. Walking away from them toward my bedroom was one of the hardest things I've ever done. I love Tyson like a brother, and I have no idea how I feel about Gray. Or maybe the truth is, I don't want to think about my feelings for Gray.

Walking out of my shoes, I leave them on the floor and keep walking toward my bathroom. It's at the front of the Bereford with a spectacular view of the park and the surrounding city. There's no need to turn a light on. I've lived here for three years and know it like the back of my hand. Reaching behind me, I pull down my dress's zipper, then remove my underwear, letting it all fall to the white-tiled floor. Next, I turn on the shower and step under its spray. The icy water causes me to grit my teeth together, but it doesn't last long. Soon the hot water is washing over me. Mechanically, I soap myself up and remove any makeup with a washcloth.

Stepping out of the shower, I strain to hear any noises coming from outside my room. The only thing I can hear is my own breathing. Toweling off, I dress for sleep and crawl onto my bed's soft mattress. At first, I lay there staring at the ceiling, but this does nothing to soothe my nerves, so I sit up, fluffing pillows to put behind me. I find myself staring at my open bedroom door, wishing Gray would walk through it. Eventually, I get out of bed and pad into Dawson's room.

He has a night light next to his little bed, and I turn it on. The soft light illuminates the space, sending patterns onto the ceiling and walls. Sometimes when he can't sleep, I turn on the music box that's next to it. It feels strange to be reaching for it and putting it on without him here, but tonight, I think I need the comfort. As the twinkling music fills the air, I'm reminded how small and fragile my son is and what a mess I've made of things with Gray.

Warm hands land on my shoulders, and I'm turned into Gray's embrace. He holds me, and I breathe in his long-forgotten scent. My hands encircle him, and we sway to the music. No words are needed as we cling to each other in our son's room.

The music stops, and I pull back from him. Gray's fingers move a few strands of hair off my face, and then he puts his hand in mine and walks me back to my bedroom. Once inside, he closes the door, and I follow him toward the bed. Gray pulls back the covers, and I crawl into the middle of the bed, facing away from him. I can hear him removing his clothing, then the bed dips as his body curls in around mine. His arm goes over my hip and around my stomach, pulling me even closer to him.

Neither of us speak. We lay together in the dark, and for the first time, in a long time, I fall asleep without worrying what tomorrow will bring.

CHAPTER 20

GRAYSON

Seeing Diandra standing in Dawson's room last night, looking so lost, made me realize she's been alone with this burden. Not that our son is a burden. I understand Diandra would do anything for him, just like she thought she was doing right by me all those years ago. Maybe Tyson is right, maybe the universe has a strange sense of humor, and we both needed to change and grow to be better people for the adversities that our son now faces.

The sun has barely broken through the morning sky. I'm awake, staring at Diandra as she sleeps, nestled against me. Her hair is fanned out over the pillows, making her appear almost child-like. She moans and arches in sleep, pushing herself up against me. My cock instantly becomes hard, and my hand moves down her body. At first, I trace the curve of her hip repeatedly, but I want more. Dragging her nightie up, my hand traces along the top of her trimmed pussy, exploring her body. Diandra moans, and in her sleep, her hand finds mine, pushing it down between her folds. She grinds against my hand, and my finger seeks her small nub.

"Gray," she gasps.

Although I'm happy she calls out my name in her sleep, I feel shameful at my lack of self-control. Unable to stop myself, I continue to tease her until she's wet, and my fingers slide inside, stroking her until her pussy spasms around them. Slowly, I withdraw my hand and slide it up to her hip, where she catches and holds it to her breast. My cock is aching for her. Not wanting to control my desires, my hand fondles her breast, massaging it until her nipple pebbles. My lips lock onto her earlobe, and I kiss and suck it, working my way down her neck. Dee rolls over, her eyes still closed, giving me unfetted access to her body. Her legs apart, and I want so badly to bury myself in her, but for that, I need her to be awake.

Dee's eyes crack open, and my hand is cupped around her breast. She reaches up and pulls my head to hers, kissing me wantonly. Reaching down, I pull the nightie up and over her head. Her legs part further, and I move between them. But instead of burying my ever-hard cock inside her, I kiss my way down her body. I take in the stretch marks that have changed her from a girl into a woman. I marvel at this new body, a body that I once knew so well and now get to discover all over again.

Dee moans as I suck on her nipple, only to leave it and move further down. She whimpers when I suck on her clit and insert a finger into her, stroking and eliciting a long, low purr. Dee's hands latch into my hair, and her legs go over my shoulders as she grinds herself onto my face. The taste of her is like honey, and I lap at her until she cries out, and I feel her spasm around my fingers again.

I wipe my face on her sheets, then I gradually trail kisses up her body until I reach her mouth. This I claim. My tongue dives into her, and my lips punish hers. With our hands intertwined, I ease myself inside of her, my muscles straining so I don't crush her underneath my weight. Dee breaks the kiss, her head moving to the side as I withdraw and ram back into her. With her eyes closed, Dee has her mouth slightly open as I do it again, except this time her hips match my movement. Her eyes open, and she turns her head to stare intently at me as I pump into her.

"Please," she begs, then pulls on one of her hands.

Immediately, I release it, and she moves it down between us, working herself as I move in and out of her.

It takes only a moment, and her body quivers with the orgasm that rocks through her. The extra pressure on my cock electrifies me, and I grunt as I spill my seed inside of her. The orgasm hits me hard, and for a moment, I think it's never going to end as I lose myself, once again, in this woman.

I'm breathing hard, gazing down at her. Dee's one free hand tracks up my stomach to clasp around my neck, where she pulls me down for a kiss. This kiss is soft and sweet. I let her guide it, not pressuring her for more than she wants to give. When she eventually breaks the kiss, I roll off and out of her, laying next to her in the early hours of the morning light.

Dee pulls the sheet up between us, covering her body. I move to my side, tracing patterns on her upper arm, not saying anything, simply enjoying the feel of her in our post-consummation in this new chapter of our lives.

Dee's hand moves to lift my chin, so I'm staring into her eyes. "Are you okay?"

I smile at the concern in her voice as though she made the first move when all along it was me.

"No, I'm not." A frown creases her radiant face, and I reach up to smooth it out. "Everything is perfect. The way it's meant to be."

The frown disappears, replaced with a smile, and she holds my hand to the side of her face. Leaning down, I kiss her and then roll onto my back. Dee comes with me, her head on my chest and one of her legs over mine.

My hand once again traces patterns on her back, and Dee lies on top of me. Soon, one of her hands explores my body, going further down until she grasps my cock. My head arches back into the pillows, and I hiss as she strokes me.

Dee kisses my chest, then moves to straddle me. Leisurely, she lowers herself onto my cock. The first roll of her hips has me digging my nails into the soft skin of her buttocks. Rising, I press myself into her further as she rides me. Her nails dig into my chest, and I move her faster. Dee's eyes never leave mine, both of us working our way to another release. While one hand holds onto her hip, the other uses my thumb to press on her clit. Dee increases her speed and moans louder, digging her nails further into me.

The pain combined with being buried this far inside her is too much. My balls tingle as I come, then Dee cries out as her pussy spasms around my cock, milking me, drawing out another long orgasm for us both. When it's finally over, Dee collapses on top of me.

My hands are limp on the bed, and as the sun creeps through the windows, I fall back asleep with my cock, firmly planted within this magnificent woman.

When I wake, the bed is empty. I rise on my elbows, but she's not in the room. Throwing back the sheet, I walk through her bedroom to her bathroom, but she's not there. I check the other bathroom that adjoins her and Dawson's room, but she's not in there, either.

Turning on the shower, I wash myself down. The nail marks on my chest are a happy reminder of what we did earlier. When I'm done, I walk through Dawson's room and into the bathroom next to my room and quickly dress.

I find Dee in the kitchen, standing in front of the coffee maker, her expression a million miles away from where we are right now.

"Good morning." The words come out as a loud whisper, and she jumps at the sound.

Turning, Dee dashes over and places her arms around me. "Good morning."

"You should've woken me up."

Dee leans back and looks up at me. "You were peaceful in sleep, so I didn't want to disturb you."

"Dee, you can disturb me anytime. We have a lot to catch up on."

"Do you mean that?"

I nod. "I've never meant anything else more."

Looking around the kitchen, I ask, "Where are Tyson and my mom?"

"They're both at the hospital. Your poor mom has been there all night."

"She won't mind," I assure her.

"Oh, don't I know it. She told me on the phone not to worry about it, that she was perfectly fine, but I've spent enough nights in those chairs to know it's a lie. Her spirit might be willing, but the flesh will be in agony trying to get comfortable."

"We should probably go, then?"

Dee nods but doesn't move. "Yes, we should but not until you eat something."

Guiding me toward the kitchen island, she has a selection of fruit, toast, and muffins on it for me to choose from. Dee kisses my cheek, releases me, and pours two coffees. We sit side by side on the stools as we eat. There's so much I want to say to her, but this morning feels magical, and I don't want to break the spell. Almost as if she can hear my thoughts, Dee clears her throat, and we stare at each other.

"What are we doing?" she asks.

"Getting to know each other again."

Dee smiles. "There's no easy way to say this, but here goes. I can't have you half in my life. Dawson adores you, but he doesn't really know you. He won't understand if you aren't going to be here full-time."

"Do you have to be here?"

"As in this apartment or New York?"

"Both."

"My agency is here. My mom moved back here to be close to us. I'm not sure I want to give any of that up."

"Your dad still lives here?" Dee nods. "We can't live here in Tyson Reed's apartment."

"Do you know how expensive it is to buy in New York?"

"That bad, huh?"

"Yes."

"How much does a place like this cost?"

"Tyson paid twenty-five million for it, and he got it at a ridiculous price. It's worth more like forty million now, but at the time, the owners were desperate. They invested badly in a few deals and needed to recoup money quickly, so Tyson cashed in and got it for a steal."

"Forty million?" I repeat, with my mouth hanging open.

"Yep," Diandra replies, smacking her lips together.

"There must be cheaper places to buy or rent." Dee nods. "Well, we don't need to move immediately. We can look."

"You're willing to move here?"

"Yeah, and I bet Mom would come too."

Dee leans into me and puts an arm around my waist. "Thank you."

"We don't need to decide this right now, though, do we?"

Dee puts her chin against my arm. "No, we don't. It's enough to know you'd move here for us."

Looking into her eyes, I say, "In a heartbeat. Nothing is ever going to separate us again. No more running. From now on, we'll face every adversity together, head-on, as a team."

Dee smiles at me, her blue eyes shining with happy tears.

Those words would come back to haunt me in the months that follow.

CHAPTER 21

GRAYSON

The steady beeping of a machine brings me out of my slumber. Opening my eyes, I see my mother hovering above me, a look of concern on her face.

"Nurse!" she yells, "He's awake."

I reach up, and something covers my face. I pull on it, and my mother holds my hands.

"Grayson, wait for the nurse."

"Sleeping beauty is awake?" asks a voice as she, too, stands over me.

My mother looks anxious as she holds my hands, staring at the woman.

"Grayson, do you know where you are?" The nurse shines a light in my eyes, and I flinch.

"H-hospital," I croak out.

"Yes. Can you tell me your date of birth?"

"F-February eighth."

Pulling one of my hands out of my mother's takes much effort. I touch my throat and then pull at the mask on my face, but my hand and arm feel strange.

"Can he do that?" asks mom nervously.

The nurse nods. "My name is Rachel. You gave us quite a scare." She hits a button, and the bed moves into a better sitting position. "Your throat might be sore. We intubated you. How does it feel?"

"Dry."

She smiles at me and picks up a cup with a straw in it, pulls the mask further down, and holds the straw to my lips.

The cold liquid is like heaven in my throat.

"How long?"

"Let me get a doctor to answer your questions." Rachel smiles down at me and leaves the room.

Turning to my mother, I repeat my question, "How long?"

"You've been in and out for nearly eight weeks."

"What happened?"

"You developed breathing issues during the surgery. For a while, it was touch and go."

"Dawson?" I whisper.

Mom's face lights up. "He did fine. He's put on so much weight while you've been sleeping. Diandra has had a full-time job trying to keep him still. Dawson doesn't like taking the anti-rejection medicine, but he does take it. They've been in every day to see you." Mom is still holding my hand. "How do you feel?"

I search my body, mentally feeling for injury and find none. Reaching under the bed covers, I touch my stomach, and apart from a little tenderness, it feels fine.

"I'm okay, Mom."

Relief washes over her face. "Thank the Lord." She bends and kisses my forehead. "I need to phone Diandra."

Dr. Otto walks in, a huge smile on his face. "Well, well, well, you finally wake up!" He, too, shines a light into my eyes. "How do you feel?"

"Fine." Scrubbing a hand over my face, it feels strange to feel stubble. Normally, I'm clean-shaven. I shake my head a few times to clear it. "A little groggy."

"You gave us quite a scare."

I chuckle at him and wonder if that phrase is something they teach all medical staff. "So I've been told."

Dr. Otto nods. "You're attached to a catheter, so we'll need to remove it and then get you on your feet." He moves the bed sheets back and moves the hospital gown out of the way. "Your incisions are healing nicely."

"Incisions?"

"Once you started to have a hard time breathing, it was imperative to get the kidney out as quickly as possible. As a consequence, you have a number of small incisions and a larger one about twelve inches long under your ribs. But it's healing nicely."

Looking down, the wound has already knitted itself back together, and I only have a red line. The other cuts are barely noticeable.

"It looks fine, Doc."

He nods, smiling to himself. "Of course, it helped that you're in top physical condition."

I hadn't noticed Mom leave the room, but she walks in and smiles at Dr. Otto.

"Is he okay?"

"He's fine."

"When can he come home?"

"In a day or two." Dr. Otto looks down at me. "You might have a little trouble walking at first. Eight weeks is a long time not to use your legs."

Dee bursts through the door, and both Dr. Otto and my mother move out of the way. She launches herself at me, tears streaming down her face. "Don't you ever do that to me again!"

Awkwardly, I move both my arms, and they feel like jello as I try to get them to wrap around her. It's the strangest feeling as though they know what they need to do but can't.

"I'm okay, Dee," I whisper.

Her tear-stained face searches mine. "I was so worried." She glances at mom. "We all were."

"Dawson?"

Dee smiles. "He's outside with Tyson. I was worried it was going to be like before when you went back to sleep."

"I've been awake before?"

Dee nods, and Dr. Otto clears his throat, gaining all of our attentions.

"It's common in coma patients. You were in and out. This time is different, you're wide awake and don't look sleepy."

The fog that was clouding my mind when I first woke has cleared, and I feel well-rested, not tired at all.

"Can Dawson come in to see him?"

"Of course. We need to get Grayson up and moving, but I'll give you all a few minutes alone."

Dr. Otto walks out of the room, and I look anxiously at the door, waiting for Dawson to walk through. But it's not my son who stumbles through the open doorway, but my best friend, Colton Anders.

He moves to the opposite side of the bed, looking as upset and distressed as Diandra first did.

"You scared me, Gray," Colt chokes out, and my mom puts an arm around him.

"Sorry, man, just taking a break."

Colt barks out a laugh and shakes his head. "Don't do it again."

He puts his hand in mine. I try to squeeze it, but again my muscles don't seem to know what to do. Colt doesn't seem to notice as he manhandles me and then releases me just as quickly.

"Dad?" says a small voice.

Turning my head back to the doorway, I see Dawson in Tyson's arms. I smile widely at him.

"Hey, little man, how are you feeling?"

He reaches down and pulls up his T-shirt, exposing a thin red scar that extends around his belly.

Dawson is looking down, nodding as he babbles, "I've got a scar like you. Tyson said we have battle wounds to show how brave we are." He looks up at Tyson, who nods.

"Good to see you awake, Grayson," says Tyson as he puts my son on the edge of the bed.

Dawson moves closer to me, forcing his mother to move further away. He puts his little hand in mine.

Staring at my son's smiling face, I say, "It's good to *be* awake."

CHAPTER 22

GRAYSON

A week later, and I'm out of the hospital. While I was sleeping, Dee and Dawson moved out of Tyson's apartment, much to his displeasure, and moved into a two-bedroom, one bathroom rental above a grocery store in Kips Bay.

Compared to their last home, this is small. The elevator doesn't always operate, and even though my legs and arms are now working, those stairs can be murder. I'm exhausted by the time I get to the top.

"Dad!" yells Dawson, the sound echoing off the walls of our new home. "Where are you?"

The apartment consists of four rooms—our bedrooms, the bathroom, and an open space that serves as the kitchen, dining and living room. It's not like I can hide from him.

"I'm in here," I yell back.

I am in Dee's and my bedroom. Dawson bounds in, his excitement and curiosity expand with each new day.

"Did Mom go to work?"

"She did."

169

He crawls up onto the bed and positions himself under my arm, snuggling in.

"What are we going to do today?" he asks as he flattens his palm onto mine.

"Anything we want."

"Is Uncle Colt coming?"

"No, buddy, Uncle Colt went home with Aunty Skye."

Dawson nods. "Yeah, I forgot."

I ruffle his hair, and he giggles. "Can we go home to Uncle Tyson?"

Moving into such a small apartment, it hasn't been an easy adjustment for him or Dee. Both of their bedrooms in the old place were twice the size than they are here, and there aren't a lot of rooms to explore. With Dee going back to work, I find myself taking Dawson to the park every day so he can run wild.

"Don't you like it here, buddy?"

He looks up at me. "It's okay."

"Maybe we should find somewhere else to live?"

Dawson nods. "Not above a stinky grocery store."

The stinky part is the industrial bins in the alley next to us. Dawson doesn't enjoy walking past them and often holds his breath.

I chuckle. "Yeah, nowhere near a stinky grocery store."

Dawson nods.

"You wanna help me pick somewhere?"

He twists and turns around, sitting opposite me. "Yeah."

"Let's go eat first."

Dawson rolls to the side of the bed and slides onto the floor. Throwing back the covers, I stand, and he goes running into the kitchen. I join him as he opens the refrigerator.

"What looks good?"

"Fruit!"

Peering in, I can see that Dee has already cut up some watermelon and banana for him in two separate bowls. Little man likes to eat them one at a time and doesn't like his food to touch each other.

"Sit at the table."

He runs and sits on the couch.

"No, buddy, the table."

"But I wanna eat here and watch TV," he pouts.

"Nope. Real men eat at the table, and we don't have the TV on. Come on, get your butt up here."

Dawson giggles. "You said butt."

Holding a finger to my lips, I smile. "Don't tell Mommy."

He giggles and sits at the table. "Can I have ice cream?"

I sit and look at the fruit that Dee has also cut for me. "No more ice cream for you *or me*."

Dawson puts a piece of banana in his mouth. "Not fair."

"No, it's not. But at least we get to go through it together."

"Can Mommy have ice cream?"

"She can." Dawson frowns. "Eat your breakfast."

Both of us need to adapt to a new diet. It's not that we can't have ice cream, but it's best to avoid it for the time being. A low-salt, high-fiber diet is what the doctor recommends, and we're trying to stick to it as best we can.

I've never been to Dee's work before. It's in an office building downtown. The rent alone must cost her a fortune. The elevator opens, and I push Dawson's stroller out. There's a big desk in the foyer with a woman who smiles at me while she talks on the telephone. Pushing the stroller, I smile at her and wait for her to end the call.

"Hello, how can I help you?"

"Grayson Moore to see Diandra Evergrow."

"Do you have an appointment?"

"Ahh… no. I'm her…" Looking down at Dawson, I shrug and change tactics."I mean, he's her son, Dawson."

She stands and looks down at him. "Oh, so he is! Hello, Dawson, your mommy talks about you all the time. Shall I see if she's free?"

Dawson nods, and she looks back at me.

"Thank you."

She smiles and pushes a button. "Your son and his… nanny are here."

She looks up at me. "Ms. Evergrow will be right with you."

Within moments, Diandra joins us.

"Hey." Dee kisses my cheek and then reaches down to touch the top of Dawson's head. "This is a delightful surprise." She looks at the receptionist. "Thank you, Marion."

Dee takes charge of the stroller, and I follow her into her office.

"Wow, this is nice." I whistle loudly as I look around her office.

Dee smiles and unbuckles Dawson. He runs straight to her window and looks out.

"It is. We're doing very well."

"You must have a lot of clients?"

"We do."

Dee wraps her arms around my neck and smiles up at me. My arms instantly go around her waist.

"Marion called me your nanny."

Dee laughs. "Should I have told her you're my boyfriend?"

The idea of me being something so not permanent as a boyfriend feels wrong, and I shake my head.

"My baby daddy?"

"I hate that."

"You don't want to be Dawson's father?"

"I *am* Dawson's father." I pull her in for a kiss. "But I want to be more than a *boyfriend* to you."

"What do you want me to be?"

I cup her face in my hands. "I made a promise to you once."

Dee smiles and moves out of my embrace. She opens the top drawer of her desk and pulls out a necklace. On the end of it is a gold band. Dee takes it off the necklace and leaves that in the drawer. She holds it out to me on her palm.

"This promise?"

I take the ring off her and laugh. "You know, at the time, I thought this was beautiful."

"It is beautiful!"

I shake my head and smile at her indulgently. "Woman, it's tacky."

Dee takes it off me, puts it on her ring finger on her right hand, and holds it up. "Well, I love it."

"It's on the wrong finger."

Dee cocks her head to the side. "What are you saying, Gray?"

"I'm saying I love you, and I want to make you mine." I pull her close to me. "Marry me, Diandra Evergrow."

Dee nods and throws her arm around me. "Yes!"

I kiss her softly. Dawson taps me on the leg. I break the kiss but keep her in my embrace.

"What's up, little man?"

"Did you tell Mommy about our new home?"

Dee cocks her head to the side. "New home?"

I let her go and pick up Dawson. "We went and had a look at some larger apartments today."

Dawson nods. "Dad says rent money is dead money."

"Is that so?"

Dawson nods at her.

"Did you find anything?"

"We looked at a couple." I put Dawson down, and he runs back to the window. "Real estate in New York is expensive."

"It is," agrees Dee. "For what we pay here for an apartment, we could get a single-family home for half the price. Maybe even less."

"You'd move to Boston?"

"I've made some inquiries and reached out to James Brookes, my old boss. He's interested in selling the Boston accounting firm."

This makes me happy. I like New York, but I love Boston. All my friends are there as well as the New England Warriors. Boston is home.

"I love you."

Dee smiles. "Not as much as I love you."

CHAPTER 23

GRAYSON

I'm in the hotel room with Colt fussing over my tie. It won't sit the way I want it to. Colt walks over and undoes it.

"I keep telling you, you're not doing it right."

"Why does yours look so good?"

He pulls up my shirt collar and pulls on the ends of it, then sticks his tongue out the side of his mouth and ties the silk material into a double Windsor knot.

"Because, my friend, I've had practice. The trick is to make sure your tie lines up with your belt buckle, no gap. It looks awful if there's a gap."

Colt puts my collar down and steps away with a bow and flourish in front of the mirror.

Scrutinizing myself, I smile. "You did it."

"Was there any doubt?"

"I just want everything to be perfect."

Colt chuckles. "No one is going to be looking at you, anyway. They'll be staring at the bride and me, of course."

I slip on my coat. "*Dee* will be staring at me."

"Oh, right, her? I forgot she was coming," teases Colt.

There's a knock at the door, and my mom comes in. Her hand flutters to her throat, and she bursts into tears. "Oh, look at my boys!"

Colt puts his arm around me. "Do we look good?"

Mom comes over and puts a hand on either of us. "You both look very handsome."

"Thanks, Mom."

She looks from me to Colt and back again. "Are you ready?"

"I've been ready for ages, but your son has taken forever. You'd think he was nervous or something."

I scowl at my best friend, then smile at my mom.

"We're ready."

The wedding is being held in a park near the river, and the reception is in the restaurant downstairs. It too overlooks the river.

"Well, let's get this show on the road." Mom claps her hands.

"How are you getting to the wedding?" Colt asks her.

"I'm going with the bridesmaid."

I kiss her cheek, and so does Colt.

"Remember, you're supposed to be there early. It's only the bride who's allowed to be late."

"We know, Mom."

"Now that princess here has his tie on properly, we're ready to go."

Mom shakes her head at Colt, kisses me again, and leaves us.

"You ready to go?" I ask him.

"I was born ready."

All the New England Warriors' players are sitting in white chairs with their respective wives and girlfriends. The press is being held at bay by a sea of security guards. Colt is standing next to me, waving and smiling at the people in the crowd. He's so relaxed while I'm a bundle of nerves. The celebrant clears his throat. "Gentlemen, I've just been advised that the bride is here. Could you both face me until the music starts?"

Colt grins at me then faces forward. I scan the crowd and see my mom as she makes her way to her seat. She gives me a small wave, and then I turn around too.

It feels like I have a kaleidoscope of butterflies in my stomach. I have no idea how Colt is managing to look so calm.

The music starts, and we both turn around. Coming up the aisle is Dawson. He's holding one side of a basket with the flower girl, and they are both reaching into it and dropping rose petals on the ground.

He's practiced this for weeks. His face is a mask of concentration as he slowly makes his way up the aisle. Next comes the bridesmaid, who looks resplendent in a deep red, floor-length gown with a split in the front, revealing a lot of leg.

"Here Comes the Bride" music begins to play. It feels like everyone is holding their breath. At the end of the red carpet is the bride with her dad. Colton gasps, and although I understand his reaction, it's hard for me to take my eyes off Dee. The deep red accentuates the color of her skin. She looks more than beautiful. I watch as she stands opposite me, her eyes never leaving mine.

When the bride and her father make it to us, it breaks my line of sight to Dee, and I finally take in Skye. Her blonde hair is pulled away from her face and hangs in curls down her back. The dress isn't white but a champagne color that suits her complexion. It clings to her curves and falls gracefully to the floor. Glancing at my best friend, he's got tears in his eyes.

He shakes Skye's dad's hand and then, as if she's made of glass, carefully takes both of her hands in his. The celebrant begins his speech, and I find myself once again lost in the vision that's Dee.

She takes my breath away.

The engagement ring, a large tanzanite emerald-cut stone surrounded with diamonds, shines in the light, letting everyone know Dee is mine.

Colt nudges me, and I look at him. "The ring?"

"Oh!" I pat my pockets, and a look of terror goes over his face. I wink at him and pull it out of my coat pocket.

The audience chuckles, and Colt looks relieved. When I look back at Dee, she shakes her head, a huge grin on her face.

The celebrant announces, "You may kiss the bride!"

The guests stand and cheer. Skye reaches up and wipes the tears from Colt's face. Nothing but love radiates from the couple. As they walk down the red carpet, our teammates line the aisle blowing bubbles at them.

It's funny to see such big men doing this, but it's what Skye wanted and whatever she wants, Colt delivers.

I move to stand next to Dee. I kiss her and then hold up her hand, lean back and take in all of her gorgeousness.

"You look stunning."

Dee blushes. "So do you."

Dawson pushes between us, and we both take one of his hands and walk down the aisle together as a family.

EPILOGUE

GRAYSON

Dee is on the dance floor with Dawson in her arms. The bride and groom have long since gone. I'm amazed that little man is still awake. My mother is also on the dance floor with Skye's dad. The way she's looking at him, you'd think he was the most engrossing human being on the planet. She laughs a little too hard at his jokes, and as soon as the formal part of the day was over, they've spent every moment together—he even made sure she was sitting next to him at the reception.

"Penny for your thoughts?" asks Dee.

"Are you seeing what I'm seeing?"

"Your mom looking happy?"

I smile at her and shake my head. "Yeah, I guess so."

Dee chuckles. "Come on, Gray, time to get this little guy home."

Holding out my hands, Dawson immediately wants me to carry him. We walk out of the reception room to the elevators and up to our room. Dawson falls asleep on the trip.

Dee lovingly strokes his head. "He did so well today."

"Yes, he did. Although he didn't think much of the flower girl."

Dee bursts out laughing and then holds her hands over her mouth to stop herself from making too much noise.

"She tried to kiss him. He didn't like that *at all*."

I grin at her. "Let's put him to bed, he's had a rough day."

Dee giggles and helps me undress him. We booked a suite with a king-size bed and had them put a single bed in our room for Dawson. He doesn't wake as Dee puts a teddy bear in bed with him, and I pull up the covers, then we leave the room and head for the couch.

I take off my jacket, the tie was long ago discarded, and drape it over an armchair. Dee steps out of her heels and scrunches her toes into the carpet, making a moaning sound.

"That bad, huh?"

"Yes and no, it's just good to have them off."

"Would you like a drink?"

Dee nods. "Coffee."

There's a coffee pod machine in the room, so I walk toward it and make her one. When I come back to her, she's sitting on the couch. Eagerly, Dee holds up her hands to take the hot drink off me.

"Will you be able to sleep?"

"Coffee doesn't keep me awake."

I sit next to her. "Have you had a good day?"

"Yes. Skye was so relaxed. I was bundle of nerves, but she was fine."

I laugh. "Colt was the same." I don't admit that I too was nervous today.

"Must be true love." Dee shakes her head. "Do you remember how many girls he dated in college? I never thought he'd settle down." Dee lowers her voice. "And I never thought he'd get a nice one like Skye."

Chuckling, I say, "She had him from the moment they met, only he didn't know it yet."

Dee sips her coffee as I reach into my pants pocket and pull out the pendant she gave me so many years ago. Holding it up, her brow furrows as she tries to see what it is. Recognition goes across her face, and she reaches for it. "You still have it?" She turns it over and smiles as she looks at the engraving on the back.

I nod. "It was from you. I even have that sweater you gave me."

Dee laughs. "Do you wear it?"

"Not very often. It reminded me of you, and I missed you."

Her face turns sad, and the smile disappears. "I'm so sorry, Gray."

Reaching up, I stroke her face. "Don't be. It's all in the past."

"You've given up everything for us. It's not what I wanted."

"I know that, Dee." Taking her hand in mine, I raise it to my lips and kiss her knuckles. "You did the right thing at the time. I wasn't ready to be a father. I was so hung up on my life plan, I don't think I could have accepted a change. At the time, I thought I would have done anything to keep you, but in hindsight, I wasn't ready."

"You'd worked so hard to get a scholarship and then to get into the pro league, I didn't want to ruin it for, you but in the end, I did, didn't I?"

Shaking my head vigourously, I say, "No, no, no!" I smile and chuckle. "You made my life better. You gave me a son, and you moved here to Boston. It's you who's given up everything."

"Except you can't play ball anymore, and I know you wanted to."

"Not going to lie, it's going to be a rough transition. But I've had three good years. Football was always a short-term goal. I've achieved that."

Dee sips her coffee. "What now?"

I raise my eyebrows up and down and smirk at her. "Do you remember Lochlan MacKenny?"

"The model? He's not someone you forget easily." I growl at her, and she shakes her head. "I simply meant, he's good-looking."

"You are not making this any better."

Dee laughs. "I only want you." As if to prove the point, she holds up her engagement ring.

"Loch has a plan. He wants to open a clinic here in Boston for sports medicine, and he wants me to be a part of it."

"Does he want you to work for him?"

"No, more than that. Loch wants me to invest. This will be the first of many. It won't only be a clinic, it will also be a gym, an all-around health center. He has plans to open them across the country."

"Why does he want you?"

"I'm going to be the face of the business. Loch has it all planned." I sit up a little straighter. "The man who gave up his dream to save his son and now wants to help others." I put an arm around her. "There's a lot of money to be made in the health sector... athletes who need to be rehabilitated or need help with training, and then there's the everyday person who wants to lose weight, get toned, feel better about themselves. We've even talked about having a whole health approach and having a team of mental health professionals, which I think is a great idea. Football can be a mind fuck. If your head isn't in the right frame of mind, you've lost before the game even starts."

"Which is the same for everyone, not just athletes."

I nod. "What do you think?"

"I think you're going to need a good accounting firm to help you out."

Laughing, I pull her onto my lap. "I've already talked to Loch about it, and he seems to be on board with you looking after that side of things." Smiling, I kiss her cheek. "Tyson is interested too. The New England Warriors have a small army of people who look after them, and he's hoping to cut costs by using us. He thinks with me there, the guys will be more receptive to it."

"It sounds like a great opportunity for all of us."

Dee rests her head against mine. "It will be. There's just one small thing I want to do before we go into business with Loch."

"What's that?" whispers Dee.

"I want you to marry me. I want you and my son to have my last name."

Dee holds up her hand and touches her engagement ring. "We're halfway there."

"I want to go all the way."

Dee smiles. "What about adding to our family?"

"Another baby?"

Dee nods. "Yeah."

"We can have as many as you want."

Dee takes my hand and presses it to her stomach and smiles. "I'm hoping for a girl this time."

My heart races. "You're pregnant?"

"Yes."

"How far along?"

"Nearly twelve weeks."

I stand, taking Dee with me and putting her on her feet. "We've got to get married, and now!"

"Honey, we've got plenty of time."

Cupping her face in my hands, I kiss her. "We've got the rest of our lives, but we need to get married before this baby arrives."

"Why?"

"Call it male pride, but I want my family to have my last name, and my children to know that I love their mother so much that I want to commit to her for the rest of my life. I want the world to know you belong to me, and I belong to you for now and always."

Dee's eyes shine with tears. "I love you."

"Is that yes?"

"Oh, honey, I'm never leaving you again with or without a wedding. You're stuck with me."

I kiss her quickly. "Together, we can tackle anything, even a new life."

THE END

Tackling Love, Book 1 in the Tackling Series

BLURB

Colton Anders

Quarterback for the New England Warriors.

Playboy, cocky, self-assured, used to getting what he wants.

Skye Hadley

Teacher at a high-profile private school.

Quiet, plays it safe, never breaks the rules.

Unexpectedly, their two worlds collide.

Colton tempts Skye one night, and she throws caution to the wind, taking him home.

Unknowingly propelling herself into a world filled with fans, media, and an abundance of unwanted attention.

The media is grueling, but their chemistry is undeniable.

Vulnerable in lust, Skye wants nothing more than to give in to her heart's desires.

With the world watching, will Colt be able to win Skye over in this fun, sports romance?

If you liked this story, you might also like:
An MC/Band of Brothers Romance
Spark: MacKenny Brothers Series Book 1
BLURB
One big secret can change everything.
A feisty waitress.
A loner with his guard up.
The attraction is mutual, but Eric must decide if he can protect the secret he holds close to his chest without destroying Cherie, or whether he must walk away from the small-town girl he's falling for.
She's a dreamer.
He's overprotective.
Are you ready for the spark?
This is a standalone book and the first in series for The MacKenny Brothers.
ALSO IN THE SERIES:
Spark of Vengeance: MacKenny Brothers Series Book 2
Spark of Hope: MacKenny Brothers Series Book 3
Spark of Deception: MacKenny Brothers Series Book 4

MORE BOOKS FOR YOU TO ENJOY:
The Savage Angels MC Series
Savage Stalker Book 1

BLURB
Isn't it funny?
How one accident can change your entire path.

I was an international rock star and the female lead singer for the Grinders, but now I'm hiding in the mountains away from everything and everyone.

That is until the President of the Savage Angels MC, Dane Reynolds, gave me a reason to feel again.

He's fierce, strong, and loyal, but someone sinister hides in the shadows.

Can Dane save Kat? Or will the savage stalker get to her first?

Savage Fire Book 2
Savage Town Book 3
Savage Lover Book 4
Savage Sacrifice Book 5
Savage Rebel (Novella) Book 6
Savage Lies Book 7
Savage Life Book 8
Savage Christmas (Novella) Book 9
Savage Angels MC Collection Books 1 – 3
Savage Angels MC Collection Books 4 – 6
The Grinders Series
Truth Book One

ACKNOWLEDGMENTS

To all the authors who help me through the hard times.
Thank you.
To my cover designer, Clarise Tan, who puts up with my
endless changes and me sending stuff at the last minute
Thank you.
To the Bloggers who share my books.
Thank you.
And to you, dear Reader, for purchasing this book. THANK
YOU.

CONNECT WITH ME ONLINE

Check these links for more from Kathleen Kelly

READER GROUP

What access to fun, prizes, and sneak peeks?

Join my Facebook Reader Group.

[Click here](1)

NEWSLETTER

What to see what's next?

Sign up for my newsletter.

[Click here](2)

BOOKBUB

Connect with me on Bookbub.

[Click here](3)

WEBSITE

[Click here](4)

---

1. https://www.facebook.com/groups/391560154326565/

2. https://www.subscribepage.com/kathleenkellyauthor

3. https://www.bookbub.com/authors/kathleen-kelly

TWITTER

Click here[5]

INSTAGRAM

Click here[6]

EMAIL

Click here

FACEBOOK

Click here[7]

---

4. https://kathleenkellyauthor.com/

5. https://twitter.com/kkellyauthor

6. https://instagram.com/kathleenkellyauthor

7. https://www.facebook.com/profile.php?id=100005859376891

ABOUT THE AUTHOR

Kathleen Kelly was born in Penrith, NSW, Australia. When she was four, her family moved to Brisbane, QLD, Australia. Although born in NSW, she considers herself a QUEENSLANDER!

She married her childhood sweetheart, and they live in Toowoomba.

Kathleen enjoys writing contemporary romance novels with a little bit of steam. She draws her inspiration from family, friends, and the people around her. She can often be found in cafes writing and observing the locals.

If you have any questions about her novels or would like to ask Kathleen a question, she can be contacted via e-mail: kathleenkellyauthor@gmail.com or she can be found on Facebook. She loves to be contacted by those that love her books.